A Down-Home Country Christmas

A Whisper Horse Novella

Nancy Herkness

Red Car Press

A Down-Home Country Christmas

Welcome to Sanctuary, West Virginia!

Holly Snedegar and Robbie McGraw made their original appearance as secondary characters in my first Whisper Horse novel, *Take Me Home*. Holly's struggle to escape from an abusive marriage plays a significant part in the plotline of that book, and many readers felt she deserved to have a happy ending of her own. So here it is! Her name cued my Muse to make it a Christmas story, especially since Holly has two young children, and we all know how magical the holiday season is for kids.

For those who have read my three Whisper Horse novels already, go to the Author's Note at the end of this novella if you'd like to know where Holly and Robbie's story fits in chronologically with the series.

If you haven't yet read the series, you might want to hold off on reading the Epilogue to this novella since it shows you the future of the characters from prior stories. You can catch up by reading the three full-length Whisper Horse novels, which are, in order:

Take Me Home
Country Roads
The Place I Belong

And now, enjoy the holidays in the mountains of West Virginia!

Read other books by Nancy Herkness

The Second Glances Series

Second To None (Novella)

The Wager Of Hearts Series

The CEO Buys In (Book 1)
The All-Star Antes Up (Book 2)
The VIP Doubles Down (Book 3)
The Irishman's Christmas Gamble (Novella)

Whisper Horse Novels

Take Me Home (Book 1)
Country Roads (Book 2)
The Place I Belong (Book 3)

Single Titles

A Bridge To Love
Shower Of Stars
Music Of The Night

CHAPTER ONE

"Mama, wake up! There's something big sleeping in the gazebo."

The bed shook under Holly. She opened her eyes to see her daughters Brianna and Kayleigh sitting on either side of her, dressed in their princess pajamas. She could see them in the light spilling into the dark room from the hallway. She glanced at the clock and groaned inwardly. It was 6:12 a.m.

"Big? In the gazebo?" Holly struggled up onto her elbows as her younger daughter Kayleigh bounced on the bed again, her long braid flopping over her shoulder. Holly stretched out and flicked on the bedside light.

"I saw it when Snowball meowed to go out." Brianna's brown eyes were wide with apprehension. She tended to take life more seriously than her nine-year-old sister. "I think it's a bear."

"A bear!" Holly bolted upright. It was December, so bears were supposed to be hibernating in their cozy dens in the Appalachian Mountains surrounding Sanctuary. If one was in the midst of the closely set houses of her neighborhood instead, there was something seriously wrong with the poor creature, and it would be dangerous. "You didn't let Snowball out, did you?"

Brianna shook her head. "No, ma'am."

Holly wriggled out from under the patchwork quilt and scooted off the bed. "Let's get the binoculars."

Pulling on her robe, she jogged down the hall to the closet, groping around on the top shelf to find the worn leather strap of her father's old binoculars case. She tugged at it, almost clonking herself on the head as the heavy case slid to the edge and tipped off the shelf.

The two girls trailed behind her as she trotted past the Christmas tree, setting several ornaments tinkling as she brushed against a branch. She halted at the sliding door that looked over her patio and the backyard where the wooden gazebo nestled amid drifts of snow, icicles dangling from the eaves of its black shingled roof. The exterior lights on her house threw deep shadows in a line of tracks churned through the snow. They came from the neighbor's backyard and proceeded right up the snow-covered steps of the gazebo. Her girls were right; something big, dark, and furry was hunkered down in their otherwise empty summertime shelter.

This was one of those times when being a single parent was tough. Had her ex-husband Frank still been around, she would gladly have sent him out to handle the bear. Maybe it would have done her a favor and eaten him.

Now she had to deal with the fearsome creature alone. She lifted the glasses to her eyes and twisted the dial, bringing the animal's blurred outline into focus. Thank goodness she had installed safety lighting after Frank's abrupt departure. At least she could see in the pre-dawn darkness.

A quick scan of the dark shape and she dropped the binoculars to hang around her neck, slumping against the chilly glass in relief. "It's a donkey," she said, grateful the animal's head was in the opening so she could see its long ears and spikey mane.

"A donkey! Let's go see it!" Kayleigh raced toward the kitchen where their coats and boots hung in the mudroom by the back door.

Tension tightened Holly's shoulders. She almost wished it had been a bear; then she could have called the police and stayed indoors without embarrassment.

However, there was no excuse for not handling the donkey on her own, even though donkeys had big teeth just like the horse that had hurt her when she was eight years old. The adults had shown her how to balance a horse treat on her flattened palm. They'd told her the horse was gentle and wouldn't hurt her. Then it tore a chunk out of her thumb and stomped its foot on the side of her sneaker, breaking her little toe and betraying her trust in both the horse and the adults. After that she decided a dog was as big an animal as she wanted to go near.

"Sweetie, we don't know if it's a nice donkey or a mean donkey." Holly lifted the binoculars again to examine her nemesis. At least it was wearing a halter, so if she got close enough she could grab it. A fist of panic closed around her throat at the thought of putting her hand near those teeth.

"Mama, we have to catch it," Brianna said, her voice tight with worry. "It might try to cross the highway and get hit by a car."

Holly sighed. She was enough of a country girl to know you didn't leave valuable livestock wandering loose. The fact that her two daughters were soft-hearted animal lovers just added to the necessity of corralling the lost donkey. She lowered the binoculars and tried to ignore the flutter of nerves making her stomach lurch. "Right. I'll just get dressed and go out and grab it."

She sent the girls off to gather carrots and a rope, and put their school clothes on. Heading back to her bedroom, she yanked on jeans, a sweatshirt, and some warm socks before she went to the mudroom to add boots and a jacket. As she pulled her gloves on, she noticed her hands were trembling.

Her sister Claire would be able to handle this. She knew a lot more about horse-like animals than Holly did. Like Brianna, Claire believed in whisper horses. She honestly thought they were special creatures you could tell your problems to, and who would help you carry the burden—although Claire's horse Willow had sure helped Brianna through the ugliness with Frank, so maybe it wasn't a crazy idea after all.

Truth be told, sometimes Holly wished she had a whisper horse to talk to. Parenting alone was such a juggling act; she had days where she didn't think she could keep all the balls in the air for another second. Glancing at the kitchen clock, she calculated she had forty-nine spare minutes to get the donkey situation wrapped up before she had to get herself and the girls ready to go to school. Thank goodness her daughters had awakened her so early. She couldn't afford to lose her job as the school receptionist, and coming in late would be a large black mark against her.

"Here are the rope and the carrots, Mama," Brianna said.

"Thanks, sweetie." Holly was embarrassed by the quaver in her voice and made a show of dropping the baby carrots into one pocket before she tied the end of the rope in a loop she hoped she would be able to slip over the donkey's head.

"Once you catch it, can we come out to the gazebo?" Kayleigh asked, reappearing in the pink corduroys and sparkly princess sweater she'd chosen for today's school outfit.

"If it's a nice donkey, you can." Taking a deep breath, Holly slid open the door. "Okay, I'm going out to catch the donkey now." She swallowed hard and stepped outside, pushing the door shut behind her without taking her eyes off the dark shape in the gazebo.

The snow was a thin layer close to the house but within a few feet Holly was sinking in up to the top of her knee-high boots. She cast a quick glance behind her to see her girls with their faces and hands pressed to the glass of the slider as they watched her from the warmth and safety of the house.

Turning back to the gazebo, she squared her shoulders. She wanted to show her daughters a strong, courageous woman instead of the scared, submissive coward Frank had brainwashed her into thinking she was. If she could stand up to her abusive ex-husband, she could face a tame donkey.

She was halfway to the gazebo when the donkey swiveled its head around to watch her, its long, fuzzy ears tipped forward. Fear crawled up her spine, and she gave a little stutter step before she forced herself to keep going.

As she got closer, the donkey stretched its neck out to sniff in her direction. Even through her dread, she had to admit it was a pretty thing, with a white nose, dark eyeliner around big liquid eyes, and huge ears outlined in deep brown with white hair inside. But it still had sharp teeth and crushing hooves.

She stopped at the bottom of the steps, shifting the rope to her left hand and rummaging around in her pocket for a carrot with her right.

"Nice little donkey," she said. Her voice cracked, so she cleared her throat. "Are you hungry? I have a treat for you." She held out the carrot on her palm, exactly the way she'd been told was safe, but wasn't.

Putting her foot on the first step, she bent forward with her hand outstretched to offer the carrot. The iced-over snow crackled beneath her boot. "I'm here to help you."

Her heart began to pound and her hand shook so hard she was afraid the carrot would roll off, as the donkey pushed out its lips to nibble the treat off the flat of her glove. She forced herself not to pull away as the donkey crunched the treat between its giant, square teeth.

Holly took another carrot out of her pocket and held it out while she slid her other foot up to the next step. One more and she would be able to grab the halter.

The donkey surged to its feet, its hooves scraping and thudding on the wooden floor. Terror spiked though her and Holly jerked backwards. Her boots slipped on the icy snow coating the steps and she felt herself falling backwards, her arms pinwheeling in an unsuccessful attempt to keep her balance. As she flew through the air, she made herself go limp in an effort to not break anything.

Her back hit first, sinking through the snow and whomping against the frozen ground. Her breath whooshed out of her, and she lay gasping like a fish on the riverbank, her gaze on the star-sprinkled sky overhead.

As she battled to get oxygen back into her lungs, the stars were blocked out by a dark silhouette with long ears. She felt the tickle of warm, grassy breath and stiff whiskers on her face as the donkey snuffled at her. Horror scrabbled at her chest, and she tried to roll away from the terrifying teeth but she couldn't move. Her body was focused on getting her lungs to function.

"Mama! Mama!" Brianna's voice came nearer with each word. Holly could hear her crunching through the icy snow.

She tried to call out to reassure her daughter and tell her to go back inside but her diaphragm wouldn't relax yet. The donkey lifted its head up and away from her to look at the new visitor.

The crunching stopped. "Hello, donkey," the little girl said before her face came into Holly's line of vision. "Mama, are you all right?"

Holly managed to move her head up and down in a nod. "Just...lost...my...breath," she gasped.

"That happens to people at Ms. Sharon's stable when they fall off their horses," Brianna said. "It goes away. I'm going to catch the donkey now."

Brianna's arm snaked across Holly's vision. The girl grabbed the frayed end of the rope dangling from the donkey's halter and led it away from her mother.

"Is Mama all right? Hello, donkey." Kayleigh's voice came from behind her. Turning her head, Holly saw her two daughters stroking the donkey's face and neck as the creature stood placidly with its eyes half-closed. Holly choked on a soundless laugh. So much for her being a strong, competent woman.

"I'm...fine." She pushed herself up to a sitting

position and sucked in several deep breaths.

"Can we keep it?" Kayleigh wrapped her arms around its neck. Holly wanted to tell her daughter to move away from the donkey before something bad happened, but she swallowed the words.

"No, silly," Brianna said, ever the older sister. "Donkeys need fields and barns to live in."

"It belongs to someone," Holly said, wobbling to her feet. "Does the halter have any kind of tag on it?"

Brianna and Kayleigh examined the braided nylon halter and shook their heads.

"Darn." Holly approached the animal. She tried to feel confident as she threaded the rope through the halter ring and tied it in a secure knot. "Let's get it back in the gazebo and tie it up." She hesitated before she added, "Then I'll call the police to find out who's missing their donkey."

She just hoped Robbie McGraw was out fighting some crime or other and not at his desk. He'd seen her at her weakest during the ugly disintegration of her marriage eighteen months before—not the image she wanted him to have of her. Now she was going to look like a clinging vine again. And heaven knew, between his mother and his sisters, he'd had enough of women clinging to him.

"Won't the donkey be cold?" Kayleigh asked.

Holly shook off her concerns about Robbie and scanned the donkey's fuzzy gray coat. "No, it'll be fine as long as it's out of the snow." She led the donkey up the steps and tied the rope to the gazebo's railing. Gingerly giving its neck a single pat, she muttered, "Good donkey."

"Look, Mama, it's got a pretty black stripe over its shoulder." Kayleigh traced the line with her finger.

"It's a Jerusalem donkey," Holly said, the knowledge popping up from some nearly-forgotten Bible school lesson. "The kind that carried Jesus into Jerusalem on Palm Sunday."

"And Mary rode one too," Brianna said. "To get to Bethlehem for Jesus to be born. We learned a song about it in church school."

"Can we ride the donkey like Mary and Jesus?" Kayleigh's face lit up with excitement.

"Not without a saddle and a bridle," Holly said.

After they'd settled the donkey in the gazebo, Holly made the girls come in to eat their breakfast. She left them at the table with their grits while she took the cordless phone into the living room and dialed the police station.

Holly thought of all the times she'd longed to call the police when Frank staggered through the door drunk and violent, but she'd been too ashamed to bring in outsiders to see what was going on in her marriage. Her ex had convinced her it was her fault he behaved that way.

"Well, hey there, Mrs. Snedegar," the dispatcher said before Holly could speak. "Let me see if Captain McGraw is here."

"No, no, wait..." But the dispatcher had already put her on hold. Holly felt the flush of embarrassment climb her cheeks and was relieved no one could see it. Would Robbie think she was using the lost donkey story as an excuse to drag him back into her life?

Robbie's deep voice came through the receiver. "Holly, is everything all right?"

"Yes, and I'm sorry. I didn't mean for them to bother you," she tried to explain. "I just called to find out who might be missing a donkey."

"You found Farmer Grady's jenny!" She heard amusement and relief in his voice.

"You mean this is the nativity donkey?" Every year, a week before Christmas, Grady Boone, an elderly widower who owned a farm near Sanctuary, set up a nativity scene with a few live farm animals in a field beside the main highway. All the children in town loved to visit the display.

"Her name's Noël," Robbie said. "A couple of good old boys got drunk last night and ran their truck into the nativity scene. The animals got loose, but we rounded up all of them except the donkey. Grady will sure be relieved to have her back. I'll bring him and his truck over to your place to load her up."

"She's tied up in the gazebo right now with a bucket of water. The girls fed her all the carrots I had in the house but she's probably still hungry, poor thing." Now that the donkey was safely captured, Holly could afford to be sympathetic.

"Sounds to me like she's pretty well taken care of," Robbie said. "I'll be there in twenty."

Holly hung up and glanced at her watch. She knew the girls wouldn't want to leave without seeing the donkey off. She went back to the kitchen. "Guess who that donkey belongs to?"

"Farmer Grady's nativity scene," Brianna and Kayleigh chorused in unison.

"We heard you when you were talking to the policeman," Brianna admitted.

"Captain Robbie is coming to pick her up, so if you want to wait and say good-bye, you have to be ready to go to school before he gets here."

"Yes, ma'am," Kayleigh said, picking up her spoon and scooping up a large dollop of the grits she'd barely touched before. "I'm glad the donkey ended up here, so Captain Robbie has to come see us."

Heaven help her, but Holly felt the same way.

CHAPTER TWO

The growl of a truck engine followed by the metallic rattle of an empty livestock trailer sent Holly racing out the front door. She watched as the door of the ancient green truck creaked open, and Robbie sprang out onto the driveway like the former athlete he was, landing lightly on thick-soled police boots. A weak sunbeam from the breaking dawn found glints of blond in his light brown hair, and she could see how blue his eyes were, even from twenty feet away.

He strode up the cement sidewalk, and her eyes were drawn to the fluid movement of his long legs in their ink-dark uniform trousers. His badge caught the sun, making her blink at the sudden flash against his winter jacket. On his face was the official "everything will be all right, ma'am" smile. It softened into something a little more personal as he got closer and she smiled back.

The truth was she'd had a crush on him when he

was the high school football team's quarterback, but she was two years younger than he and too shy to do more than worship him from afar. After he graduated he'd traded his green-and-gold Spartan's uniform for a police officer's deep blue. When Frank turned violent, Robbie had come back into her life in his professional capacity, taking responsibility for her safety until he had confirmed her ex had left the country to live in Mexico. With all her money.

He still monitored Frank's whereabouts with the promise to warn her if the bastard ever reappeared in Sanctuary. And her crush had matured into an awareness that unsettled her every time she saw Robbie.

"Morning, pretty lady," he said. Holly's heart did a little flip when he called her that. "Grady took a shy spell and sent me with his truck and trailer. He's gotten reclusive since his wife died."

"We all miss Bess Boone. She was such a sweet person." She twisted her hands together in front of her. "I've got nineteen minutes before we have to be in the car. The girls won't leave until Noël does."

"Then let's get Noël loaded." He held out his hand to help her down the slippery steps. She hesitated, looking at the long fingers she'd seen him wrap around a football and the butt of a gun. She'd also seen Robbie's hand clenched into a fist when Frank threatened her at the 4-H barn dance.

She laid her hand in his, feeling the strength of his grasp for the split second it took to reach the sidewalk. She wanted to hold onto that warm, strong anchor for the whole walk around the house to the gazebo—and beyond—but he released her as soon as she stood on the sidewalk beside him, shifting his grip to her elbow to steady her through the snow.

She reminded herself that it was just his automatic chivalry toward women in general. He had four older sisters and, up until her death two months ago, a frail and ailing mother, so he was well-trained in gallantry. His gesture meant nothing more than basic courtesy, but she was willing to take even that crumb of attention.

"Noël sure walked a long way from her farm," she said, as delicious flickers of sensation radiated from his hand up her arm through the layers of her wool coat and sweater.

"The crash probably scared her." Robbie shortened his stride to match hers. "Those two drunken idiots deserve more than a few nights in jail and a fine. Grady was pretty torn up over the destruction, since he and Bess built the nativity scene together."

"Maybe we could help him fix it up again," Holly said, sympathy tugging at her.

Robbie shook his head. "It's pretty smashed up. And he says he's done with it."

"That's a shame." Holly felt a flare of anger at the drunk driver. He'd destroyed more than just some wooden shapes. He'd destroyed a Sanctuary holiday tradition.

Alcohol had ruined many holidays for her too. She flashed back to the times Frank would bang open the door, smelling of liquor and calling out loudly for his girls to come kiss him. On those evenings, she would run interference to keep him away from Brianna and Kayleigh, which made him angry and mean. Once he even deliberately knocked over the Christmas tree, stomping on the ornaments not broken by the fall. She could hear the sound of his shoes crunching the thin, fragile glass on the wood floor; it still sent tendrils of despair winding through her chest.

"Captain Robbie! Look who came to visit." Kayleigh waved from the gazebo where she stood beside the donkey.

Her daughter's innocent friendliness pulled Holly out of the dark memories.

Brianna was stroking Noël's head and neck, but she looked up with a shy smile as they approached. "She likes being petted."

When Robbie released Holly's elbow to climb the steps of the gazebo, she felt the loss. Yet she knew she shouldn't lean on him, either physically or emotionally.

"You girls are the best donkey-sitters I've ever seen," Robbie said, untying the rope from the gazebo's railing, "but now we've got to get Noël back home." He led the donkey down the steps, the two girls following close behind.

"Can we visit her after school?" Brianna's gaze shifted between her mother and Robbie.

Holly looked at Robbie. "It depends on Mr. Boone." Her guilty hope was that the old farmer would say no. She had been looking forward to the donkey's departure, taking those big teeth and sharp hooves far away.

Not to mention the fact that Christmas was fast approaching and she still had cookies to bake for the annual church swap, donations to collect and drop off for the hospital toy drive, and her own family gift-wrapping and cooking to do. Donkey visits hadn't been factored into her schedule.

"I'll ask him," Robbie said, tramping through the snow.

As the donkey walked placidly along beside Robbie, Holly called herself every kind of coward. However, her pulse skittered when they got to the trailer and he turned to her with the rope. "Can you hold Noël while I flip the ramp down?"

"S-sure." She gripped the nylon line as though her life depended on it, even as she took a step away from the donkey. She reminded herself to project confidence, both for her daughters and for Robbie. "No problem," she said in a firmer voice.

Robbie gave her a little smile of encouragement before he began unhooking various latches. Holly's attention was split between making sure the donkey wasn't going to bite her and watching the flex of Robbie's thigh muscles outlined by his trousers as he bent and straightened while lowering the ramp.

"Mama, Noël's eating my pom-pom!" Kayleigh clutched her pink knit cap to her head as the donkey nibbled on it.

With a guilty start, Holly pulled Noël's head

away from her daughter. "Sorry, sweetie." She'd let her attention stray to Robbie's body for too long. "I didn't know donkeys liked yarn."

Robbie disappeared into the trailer, removing that distraction. While the girls cooed and hugged the donkey, he jogged back down the ramp.

"Say good-bye to Noël, girls." Holly gave the donkey's neck another brief, tentative pat before Robbie took the rope from her.

He turned to the children. "Grady will sure be grateful to all of you for taking such good care of Noël."

"Will you ask him about visiting her?" Brianna repeated, her brown eyes filled with pleading.

"I'll text your mom as soon as I get his answer," Robbie said. "Now you all skedaddle off to school or you'll be late."

Holly was as reluctant to leave as the girls, although for a different reason, but his reminder sent her scurrying for the garage with her daughters in tow. A quick glance at the mini-van's clock told her they'd be about two minutes late.

Sometimes she hated that darn clock.

Robbie watched Holly and her girls disappear into the garage. He'd gotten attached to the quiet, serious Brianna and her sassy little sister Kayleigh. They seemed miraculously unscarred by the ugliness their father had put the family through with his abuse and desertion. Holly was one heck of a good mother.

Holly's mini-van rolled backward down the short driveway and onto the street, the two girls waving madly. He lifted a hand in response. Through the windshield, he saw Holly smile and bob her head to him as she steered past Grady's rig. That sunshine smile of hers always gave him a little kick in the chest.

Then she had this other smile he'd catch sometimes when she looked at him, a kind of secret, sideways slant of eyes and lips that made him want to sink one hand into her dark, silky-looking hair and use the other one to pull her curvy body up against him while he tasted her soft mouth. That was the smile he waited for, and knew he shouldn't.

"Come on, Noël, let's get you home." He gave the rope a tug as he started toward the ramp.

One step and he was jerked to a stop by the taut line in his hands. Glancing back, he saw Noël had her front feet planted wide apart, her neck stretched out full-length. He knew the proper way to load livestock into a trailer from summers of working on his uncle's farm, but his focus had been on fantasies he shouldn't be contemplating. "Sorry, girl. Let's try it again."

He positioned himself beside the little beast's head, grasped the cheek strap of her halter, and turned her away from the trailer ramp in a tight circle, getting her walking before he pointed them both back at the trailer.

One foot from the ramp, Noël planted her hooves and stopped again, fighting the forward pressure he put on her halter.

"What's bothering you about the trailer?" he asked, leading the donkey to one side of the ramp and tying her to a ring so she could see into the vehicle.

Maybe Noël didn't like the sense of walking into an enclosed space. He looked up at the mountains crowding the horizon. He knew about feeling trapped. After graduating from West Virginia University, he'd landed a job with the Chicago police department where he was on the fast track to becoming a detective. A year later, his father had died, and his ailing mother asked him to come home. He didn't regret helping his mother out during the last years of her life but now that she was gone, he'd soon be busting out of the confines of Sanctuary.

That's why he had to keep his hands off Holly. She wasn't the kind of woman you loved and left.

And there was no chance she was leaving Sanctuary. She'd often told him how important it was to her and her children to have the support of her sister, her friends, and the whole community.

He brought his gaze back to the donkey. "Okay, watch me." He walked up the ramp and stepped into the trailer, fluffing the fresh straw bedding Grady had pitchforked into the trailer at the farm. "Think of it as a nice, comfortable temporary stall."

He wished he had some of those carrots the girls

had been feeding her, but she'd come along so agreeably until now that he didn't think he'd need treats to entice her. And Grady had said she was an easy loader.

He walked back down the ramp and untied Noël, steering her into the same circular maneuver. "Come on, girl!" He put all his weight and momentum forward.

This time he got Noël's front hooves onto the ramp before he was yanked backwards, nearly falling as he lost his balance on the sloped surface. He flailed a moment before his arm found the donkey's sturdy back, and he used her to right himself.

Putting his hands on his hips, he surveyed Noël. She couldn't weigh more than three hundred pounds but she had a heck of a lot of leverage with those four legs. He pulled out his cellphone with a huff of frustration. "Hey, Pete, can you come over to Holly Snedegar's house on Cornsilk Lane and give me a hand with a donkey?"

As soon as Pete stopped laughing, he agreed to head over, arriving fifteen minutes later.

"You can't get that little critter up a ramp?" Pete said, as he climbed out of the police car, his ruddy face alight with amusement at Robbie's predicament. He rubbed a hand over his crew-cut blond hair and chortled. "Wait until I tell the rest of the guys about this."

This was one of the problems with having your best friend and former teammate as a partner. No respect, even though Robbie outranked him. "Tell you what. I'll let *you* handle this." Robbie handed the rope to Pete before he stood back and crossed his arms over his chest.

After Pete's three attempts to get Noël on the trailer, Robbie was doubled over with laughter. "At least I got her hooves on the ramp." His amusement died when he realized his new job in Atlanta would mean not seeing Pete anymore.

"I've met mules less stubborn than this critter," Pete said, wiping away sweat from his forehead.

"Looks like a two-man job," Robbie said. "I'll take the head. You get behind and push."

"How about you take the rear and I'll stay up here?"

Robbie shook his head. "What kind of a captain would I be if I didn't lead the charge?" He held out his hand for the rope, and Pete grudgingly passed it over.

"If I get kicked, I'm sending you the doctor bills." Pete put his hand on Noël's back and sidled up to her hind end with caution.

"Grady says she doesn't kick or bite." Robbie grinned. "But Grady also said she was easy to load." He wrapped his fingers around Noël's halter. "On three. One…two…three."

Robbie threw his weight forward as he heard a grunt of effort from Pete. Noël's body rocked and her hooves skidded a few inches forward. "Again," Robbie commanded, giving it his all. Noël threw her head up and let out a long, honking bray that made his eardrums feel like someone was pounding on them with a hammer.

"What the—?" Pete stopped pushing and straightened up. "This donkey just does not want to go in there." He looked Noël over, just the way Robbie had earlier. "If we got a couple of more guys, we could probably pick her up and carry her on."

"I've got a better idea," Robbie said. "I'm taking Noël back to the gazebo and leaving her there until lunchtime at school. Then we'll get the donkey whisperers back here for a quick load."

"Donkey whisperers?" Pete shook his head. "You been talking to Sharon Sydenstricker up at Healing Springs Stables too much. Her and her whisper horses, thinking there's a horse who'll listen to your problems and make them all better."

"There are some smart people in town who swear by their whisper horses, including Holly's sister Claire." Robbie put a note of warning in his voice.

Pete held up his hands. "No offense meant. I'm just sayin'."

"I know what you're saying." Robbie just didn't know what to say back. He thought Sharon's theory was crazy too. "Wait here. You can give me a ride back to Boone's to pick up my cruiser." He gave Noël's lead line a tug. The donkey looked at him without moving. "Pete, close the back gate of the trailer, would you?"

"You let me know if you need any help leading the itty bitty donkey around the house." Pete smirked as he swung the gate closed.

Robbie said something rude to his partner before he took hold of Noël's halter and steered her around the side of the trailer. The little beast stepped forward without hesitation, and they made the trip to the gazebo in amicable silence. After filling the water bucket, Robbie double checked the knot he'd tied Noël with, and gave her a pat on the shoulder. "I can't say I blame you for wanting to hang around Holly and her girls. I get tempted myself."

CHAPTER THREE

Holly was squashed up against Robbie's side on the bench seat of Grady Boone's battered pickup, with Brianna and Kayleigh sharing a single seatbelt beside her. Even through Robbie's wool police jacket she could feel the heat and muscle of his body, making warmth ripple through her own. It would have been one of the best rides of her life except that Robbie had done his withdrawing act again. Every time she felt like they'd made a connection, the "protect and serve" mask would drop over his face, and he'd pull away.

"Mama, does Noël look okay?" Brianna twisted around, trying to see the donkey tied in the trailer behind them.

"I can see her in the rearview mirror," Robbie said. "She's doing just fine. She's an old pro at this."

"Once you get her in the trailer," Holly muttered. It had taken all four of them to persuade Noël to trot up the ramp. Thank goodness Brianna's teacher had volunteered to take over Holly's lunch duties when she heard about the nativity donkey.

"She didn't want to give up all the attention she was getting from the beautiful Snedegar ladies," Robbie said.

Holly flushed with pleasure even though she knew Robbie was just being sweet to the girls.

Kayleigh giggled. "Mama's beautiful. We're just pretty."

"Do you think Noël's lonely at Mr. Boone's?" Brianna turned toward Robbie.

"It's a possibility." He downshifted as they approached the turn onto the farm's gravel road. Holly felt the muscles in his thigh flex against hers as he moved his foot between the clutch and the accelerator.

To their right a set of tire tracks veered off the highway, went straight to a hole smashed through the fence, and drew two parallel lines up a slight slope to the now-ruined nativity scene. The roof of the stable tilted crazily to one side where the supporting column had been smashed. The painted wooden figures were scattered over the ground like fallen chess pieces. The bottom half of the Virgin Mary's blue gown still stood upright while her top half had disappeared in a heap of splintered wood.

"No wonder Mr. Boone feels too discouraged to put it back together," Holly said.

"There's not going to be a nativity scene anymore?" Brianna's voice was laden with distress.

"We'll see," Robbie said. "Right now Mr.

Boone's still upset about the damage."

"But this is where everyone goes after church on Christmas Eve," Kayleigh said. "I see all my friends here."

The practice had started with Bess Boone offering hot chocolate and cookies from her kitchen to a few children whose parents had driven them up to see the nativity scene. Back then it had a live horse, sheep, goat, cow, and chickens, as well as the donkey. As Grady got older, he kept fewer and fewer animals on the farm, so he'd replaced the live creatures with wooden replicas, except for Noël, the cow, and the chickens.

But more and more parents brought their children there to wish each other a merry Christmas after the various evening church services, and it grew into a full-blown Sanctuary tradition. When the crowd got too big for Bess to handle on her own, a battalion of mothers had set up urns of hot chocolate and trays of cookies in the backs of pickups. The police set up safety barricades and directed traffic, the flashing lights of their cruisers adding to the festive atmosphere.

As the old truck rattled over the rutted gravel, Holly thought about the happy greetings that were called out as each new car parked along the road and disgorged children bundled in puffy jackets, knitted caps, and mittens. Even the teenagers came along, pretending they were only there because their parents made them come, but grabbing a cookie and slouching against the fence farther down the road as they compared tunes and games on their smart phones. It was one of the many events that bound the people of Sanctuary into a community.

"Mama, can't we help him fix the nativity scene?" Brianna asked.

Holly looked at the splintered figures and the tilted roof. She remembered all the pies she needed to bake, presents she needed to buy, and choir practices to attend, on top of the usual daily chores. "Of course, we can," she said, stroking Brianna's dark hair.

She felt Robbie's shoulder rise and fall against hers in what she knew was a sigh of resignation. Guilt nagged at her for dragging him into the job when he said, "I'll round up some friends and tackle the carpentry."

"We have to get Mr. Boone to agree though," Holly said. "It's his farm, and his nativity scene."

"I'll ask him. He'll let us," Kayleigh said with a confidence Holly envied.

Robbie steered the truck around the farmhouse toward the barn. As the old vehicle shuddered to a stop, a tall, thin man with a fringe of gray hair around his bald head emerged from the barn door. His jeans had a crease pressed down the front of each leg and his jacket was a bright blue-and-yellow plaid. His tortoiseshell glasses caught a gleam of the pale winter sun as he raised a hand in greeting.

Holly unclipped her daughters' seatbelt and the two girls tumbled out of the truck. Grady Boone took a step backward as the girls rushed toward him.

"Brianna! Kayleigh! Mind your manners!" she called, leaping out of the door. She remembered that the Boones had never had kids of their own.

She caught up with the girls as they skidded to a stop in front of Grady. "Can we come visit Noël every day?" Kayleigh asked.

"We want to rebuild your nativity scene for you," Brianna said.

Holly put a hand on each of her daughters' shoulders and gave them a gentle squeeze.

Brianna glanced up at her with an apology in her eyes before holding out her hand to the older man. "I'm Brianna. Pleased to meet you."

Grady hesitated a moment before he folded his knobby fingers carefully around Brianna's small hand. "Same here."

"I'm Kayleigh Jane Snedegar." She stuck out her hand. "We love Noël."

Grady released Brianna's hand and took Kayleigh's even smaller one. "Noël's a good donkey."

"Hello, Mr. Boone." Holly held out her own hand. "I'm—"

"Holly Snedegar," the farmer said, taking her hand with more confidence than he had the children's. "I remember you from past Christmases. I reckon I should thank you for puttin' up Noël in your gazebo."

"We're so sorry about your nativity scene," Holly said. "As Brianna mentioned, we wondered if we could fix it up again for you. It would be a shame to let a drunk driver ruin such a wonderful holiday tradition."

"That's a nice offer but sometimes the Lord tells you in His own way when it's time to let things go." Grady shoved his hands into his jeans pockets as though to keep from shaking any more hands.

Robbie strolled up to stand beside Holly. "Grady, I'm thinking the Lord didn't have much to do with this particular event," he said. "I've arrested Randy Viner for driving while intoxicated and without a license at least a dozen times in the past few years. He's hit almost everything else in this town, so your nativity was just next on the list."

The old man shook his head. "I almost didn't put it out this year because everything needs a new coat of paint. I just don't have the heart for it now that Bess is gone."

"We have the heart for it," Kayleigh said. "We'll come after school every day until it's fixed."

A look of panic crossed Grady's face at Kayleigh's promise of daily visits. Holly stepped in. "Sweetheart, Mr. Boone has made his decision. Let's help get Noël out of the trailer."

They walked to the back of the trailer, Holly grasping the girls' hands to prevent them from badgering the elderly farmer any further.

Robbie swung the ramp down and jogged up to untie Noël. The little donkey willingly followed him down the ramp, heading straight for Holly. "Whoa, girl, this way!" Robbie tried to steer Noël toward the barn, but the donkey just towed Robbie along with her.

As the donkey loomed closer, Holly fought back the panic clutching at her throat and stood her ground, even as the beast came within biting distance.

"Mama, you're squishing my fingers," Kayleigh complained.

"Sorry, sweetie." Holly released both girls' hands and flexed her tense fingers. Her daughters immediately began to pet Noël, giving Holly the opportunity to sidle away from the donkey. The darned creature was like a cat, sensing her fear and tormenting her with its terrifying presence.

Brianna turned to look up at Robbie. "May I try to lead her to the barn?" Surprise jolted Holly. Brianna was usually too shy to step forward in any situation, but most especially one where she was taking on an adult's job. Maybe her daughter was on her way to becoming that independent woman Holly herself wanted to be.

To Robbie's credit, he handed the lead line to the eleven-year-old child without hesitation. "I'm pretty sure you'll be better at it than I am."

Holly's heart swelled with pride in both of them.

Brianna took the lead line in her left hand and tucked her right hand through the cheek strap of the donkey's halter, making Holly shudder. "Let's go, Noël." The girl took one step toward the barn and the donkey stepped right along with her while Kayleigh skipped beside them.

"Well, I'll be." Grady took off his glasses and

polished them with his handkerchief before settling them back on his nose. He strode after the children and the donkey. "Gotta show them the right stall."

"Thank you for letting her do that." Holly turned to Robbie who stood with his hands on his hips watching the procession with a rueful smile.

He shook his head. "I was just accepting the reality of the situation. That donkey wasn't going anywhere without your girls."

Holly started toward the barn. "What a shame Grady won't let us work on the manger scene."

"I wouldn't count it out yet," Robbie said, strolling beside her.

Walking through the barn door, Holly blinked several times to adjust her eyes to the dim light before she headed toward the sound of voices. Robbie caught her wrist in a gentle grip and tugged her to a halt. "Give your girls a couple of minutes to work their magic."

"What do you mean?" Her nerve endings tingled at the spot where his fingers had found the bare skin between her glove and her sleeve.

Robbie held his finger to his lips. Once he drew her attention to his perfectly sculpted mouth, she couldn't stop wondering what it would feel like against hers.

"I think Noël loves us as much as we love her," Kayleigh's little voice piped up.

"What do you feed her?" Brianna's question was so typical. She loved to learn about the world around her.

"Hay in the winter with some oats as a treat. Grass in the summer." The farmer's voice was a low rumble compared to the children's. "Apples too. Bess said everyone needs dessert sometimes."

"I like Mama's chocolate cream pie," Kayleigh said. "It won a red ribbon at the state fair."

Robbie bent his head closer to Holly, so his breath ruffled her hair. More delicious sensations raced over her skin. "You should enter your peach cobbler next year," he murmured. "You'd get the *blue* ribbon."

Happiness suffused Holly. He remembered those evenings right after Frank left when he'd stop by after dinner, and she'd feed him one of her homemade desserts. Those half hours when they sat together at her kitchen table had been bright spots in her day.

While Robbie was there she felt safe. Even better, she felt normal. His visits gave her a reason to put on a pretty blouse and blow-dry her hair at a time when she found it hard just to get out of bed. His appreciation of her baking had given her the confidence to start selling her cakes and pies to the local restaurants, giving her a little extra income. Heck, even Adam Bosch at The Aerie had ordered her strawberry rhubarb pies to put on his menu this past summer.

The warmth died as she remembered how Robbie had stopped coming by after about two months. It was disappointing because the half hours had slowly stretched to an hour or longer.

Sometimes the four of them would end up playing board games, laughing and teasing each other. Robbie would tell them about the airplanes he loved to pilot or entertain them with a funny story about a local troublemaker. She'd thought—

Holly stopped herself right there. If wishes were horses, beggars would ride.

"Now that I sell my pies I can't enter the fair's contest anymore," she whispered back. "I'm considered a professional."

Kayleigh's voice interrupted their whispers. "Maybe we could bring you one of Mama's pies when we visit Noël."

There was a long silence. Holly hated to lose the pleasure of Robbie's touch but she needed to rescue Grady Boone from her daughter's persistence. Gently tugging her wrist free from Robbie's grasp, she started toward Noël's stall, halting as the farmer said, "Well, I'd be right grateful for that. I miss Bess's baking something fierce."

She felt sadness twinge in her chest.

"What kind of pie do you like best?" Kayleigh asked.

"I'm partial to mince this time of year," the farmer said.

"I don't know if Mama makes those," Kayleigh said.

"Mama can make *any* kind of pie," Brianna said with certainty.

Surprise and pleasure suffused Holly. It was good to know that her girls saw her as more competent than she saw herself. "Well, that's all the time they have to work their magic." She headed toward the donkey's stall. "I need to get us all back to school."

Robbie nodded and fell into step beside her. She stole a glance sideways at the strongly etched line of his jaw, the delicious curl of his lips in a half-smile, and the tiny lines at the corner of his startlingly blue eyes. She felt his presence in the air around her, as though the warmth of his body permeated it.

She jerked her gaze forward to where the two girls and Grady were coming out of the stall. As the farmer turned to latch the lower half of the door, Noël put her head over it, opened her tooth-filled mouth, and brayed. Holly jumped as the ear-splitting sound bounced off the walls of the barn and battered her eardrums, making her heart pound so hard her chest hurt. The creature's voice was as horrifying as its teeth.

"Good-bye, Noël." Brianna stroked the donkey's neck without flinching.

"We'll see you tomorrow," Kayleigh promised the donkey.

Grady shook his head again.

"We have to get back to school, girls." Holly shooed them toward the barn door. "Thanks for letting us come back tomorrow, Mr. Boone."

"Grady," he said.

"Grady," Holly amended with a smile. She herded the girls toward Robbie's police cruiser. He was giving them a ride back to the school.

"Mrs. Snedegar," Grady called as Robbie unlocked the car doors for them.

"Holly," she corrected, turning to find the farmer standing in the frame of the barn door with his hands dangling at his sides.

"Reckon it might be a good thing to fix up that nativity scene," Grady said. "Those girls of yours seem right fond of it."

Delight at the old man's change of heart made Holly grin like a fool. "We'll be here after school to get started."

Grady ducked his head in a nod and turned back into the barn.

As he met her gaze over the roof of his cruiser, Robbie's eyes lit with satisfaction. "You just can't say no to a kid at Christmastime."

Robbie sat at his desk, staring at the computer screen. He had a boatload of paperwork to do but his brain was still back at the elementary school with Holly. The ride to Grady's farm had been a combination of heaven and hell with her crushed up against his side in the cab of the truck, every bump and turn pressing her thigh and shoulder against his. He could smell the fresh scent of shampoo drifting up from the glossy waves of her hair, making him want to bury his face in the silky strands. When she turned to talk to him, he had a hard time keeping his eyes on the road because he just wanted to drink in her beautiful face, especially those soft, curving lips.

What was wrong with him? He was headed for Atlanta and the chance to prove he could cut it in a big city police force, even make it to detective. He didn't need any ties holding him back here in Sanctuary.

The screen went into sleep mode because he'd been motionless for so long. Muttering a curse, he jiggled the mouse as Pete stuck his head around his half-open door. Relieved by the distraction, he waved his friend toward the oak chair sitting in front of his desk.

Pete closed the door behind him, making Robbie sit up straight. He had an open door policy unless the conversation was confidential.

His friend dropped into the chair. "This is a personal matter, old buddy."

"Should we be discussing it here?"

"You got something better to do?" Pete grinned at him.

Pete hit closer to home than he knew. "I guess not," Robbie said. "Shoot."

The grin vanished from Pete's face as he sat forward and leaned his elbows on his spread knees. "Here's the thing. I'm thinkin' about asking Lori to marry me, but I don't know what to do about the ring." He ran a hand over his chin. "I mean, do I buy her one she might not like and give it to her when I propose? Or do I propose and then take her ring shopping? That doesn't seem like it would be real romantic."

Robbie rocked back in his chair. "You're asking me for advice on a proposal? You must be desperate."

"You've got a whole passel of sisters."

So Pete hadn't read his mind about Holly. Not that he had been considering proposing to her, but the two topics were closer together than he cared to admit. "It doesn't matter what my sisters would want, it matters what Lori would prefer." He thought about the strong, sassy woman Pete had been head-over-heels about for the past three years. "She's crazy enough to be in love with you, so I think she'd want you to pick out the ring. You got any ideas about what she'd like?"

"She's pointed out a ring or two she thought were pretty when we passed a jewelry store window. I just don't remember them all that well."

"Walk her past another jewelry store and pay attention to what she says this time." Robbie stood up and came around the desk to shake his friend's hand. "Lori's a good lady. If she says yes, you're a lucky man."

Pete stood up with a grin. "She'll say yes." He started toward the door but turned. "I want you as my best man. You better plan me a helluva bachelor party."

Robbie was about to give his buddy grief about being so cocky when it hit him that he would be in Atlanta at the time Pete's bachelor party would need planning. It was another one of those ties to

Sanctuary he didn't want to have to fight against. He rubbed the back of his neck. "Pete, I need to tell you something, and it can't go beyond this office."

Pete's expression turned serious. "What is it, Rob?"

"I'm leaving Sanctuary in February. I got a job in Atlanta with the police force there." Robbie shoved his hands in his pockets. "No one knows except the chief and Paul Taggart because he got me the interview."

"Holy crap! When did this happen?" Pete sat down hard in the chair.

"Couple of weeks ago." Robbie shrugged. "Look, I can still plan a helluva a bachelor party. I just wanted you to know."

"You had your mind set on getting out of here when you were younger, but I thought you'd settled in after you came back. You never talked about Chicago like you were happy there." Pete shook his head. "I guess I should have figured out you weren't putting down roots in Sanctuary since you've never taken out the same woman more than three times. That ain't easy in this town."

Robbie walked over to the small, square window and glanced out at the mountain of sand-flecked snow in the parking lot. "I've got things to prove to myself after Chicago. I was a rookie there, so I made mistakes. Not big ones, but I want to do it right this time."

"Well, that competitive streak is what made you a good quarterback. I reckon it will make you a good detective too." Pete stood up and gave Robbie a thump on the back. "I'll miss you, buddy."

Robbie's sense of impending loss was almost as physical as Pete's wallop on his back. "You too, Pete. If you want a local best man, I'll understand."

"Are you kidding me? We'll all come down to Atlanta for the bachelor party. That way no one will know what trouble we get up to."

Robbie hadn't realized how much he wanted to stand by his friend at the wedding until he nearly lost the privilege. Relief rolled through him. "Why stop at Atlanta? Let's go to Vegas!"

"Now you're talkin'." Pete gave him a mock salute and walked out the door, leaving it partly open once again.

Robbie slumped down into the vacant chair as he realized how many more good-byes like this he would have to get through. His freedom would be hard-earned.

CHAPTER FOUR

"The paint's all dried up, Mama." Brianna peered into the gallon can she'd just pried the lid off of.

Holly swallowed a groan of frustration. They'd raced home after school to change into work clothes before heading back to the Boone farm. The farmer had pointed toward his workshop in a shed attached to the barn. Then he'd muttered something about tending to the cow and disappeared in the opposite direction.

She and the girls had stopped to feed Noël some carrots before pushing open the door to the shed. The workshop was large and the tools and supplies were arranged with impressive neatness, but everything was covered with dust and cobwebs. Cans of paint lined up like soldiers on wooden shelves marked "Christmas Scene".

"Well, at least we know what colors we need to get." Holly used a stir stick to poke at the dried paint in the can she'd opened. It was as solid as a rock. She put her hands on her hips and blew out a breath as she looked around for brushes. This was going to be a bigger job than she'd thought, even with Robbie's promised help.

She jumped and spun around as the door to the shed banged open. A red-headed woman dressed in paint-spattered jeans walked in, her green eyes scanning the room. "Great light! I can work in here," she said.

"Julia?" Surprise kicked at Holly. "How did—? Never mind. Claire told you."

Julia nodded. "She thought you might need some help with the painting."

Holly swallowed hard. Only her sister Claire would send a world-famous artist to repair a simple nativity scene.

"The paint's dried up." Brianna held out the can to Julia.

"No problem," Julia said. "Hardy's Hardware is going to donate any supplies we need. Why don't you help me make a list of the colors, girls?"

Holly had just unearthed a pad of paper and pen from her tote bag when two men walked through the shed door. One went straight to Julia, wrapped his arms around her, and dipped her low for a long, dramatic kiss.

"Paul, there are children in the room," the larger man said before sauntering over to give Holly a bear hug and a peck on the cheek. "How's my favorite sister-in-law?"

She greeted her sister's giant husband Tim Arbuckle with deep affection. Tim had once faced down Holly's ex-husband Frank on a night he had spun out of control. "Overwhelmed by the size of this job until you arrived with reinforcements."

"Claire is meeting with some wealthy clients at the gallery, but she'll come as soon as she's convinced them to buy half a dozen of Julia's paintings," Tim said, releasing her.

Holly stepped back, only to be pulled into a hug by Paul Taggart, a local lawyer and former mayor of Sanctuary who ran a national organization for *pro bono* legal work. "What skills does a lawyer bring to fixing a nativity scene?" she teased.

Paul's smile flashed white against olive skin. "I'll sue the drunk driver to recover funds to pay for repairs."

Tim snorted. "So we'll have the money to do the job in what, five or six years?"

"Tim, you leave Paul alone," Holly said. "We all know he can work at high speed when it's needed." He'd pushed her divorce through so fast Frank didn't know what hit him.

Paul looped his arm over Julia's shoulders, and wove his long fingers into her mass of red curls. "Some things need to be done fast." He looked down at Julia with a wicked smile. "And some need to be done very, very slowly."

Julia flushed pink and smacked him lightly on the arm.

"Well, you're sure taking your time about

proposing," Tim said.

Julia rolled her eyes as Paul chuckled. "When the time is right," he said.

Holly heard a footstep outside the door. It was Robbie. She knew it by the electricity she felt in the air.

When he strode in, the light seemed to grow brighter and clearer, yet she could see nothing but him. He'd changed out of his uniform into worn jeans that hugged the muscles in his thighs. An olive jacket with zippered pockets hung open over a deep blue flannel shirt that brought out the azure of his eyes. His gaze went straight to her and he smiled. Not his police smile, but the one that made her forget her vow to be strong and independent.

"You're collecting helpers right and left," he said, jerking his chin over his shoulder.

Holly forced herself to unlock her eyes from him and follow his gesture. Just outside the doorway stood three of Robbie's fellow police officers, all in civvies, each carrying one of the damaged nativity figures. "Hey, Mrs. Snedegar, where would you like these?"

For a moment Holly was at a loss. They expected *her* to tell them what to do? Her gaze skittered around the workshop before she opened her mouth to ask Robbie what he thought. Then she looked at Brianna and Kayleigh who were taking in the scene from their perch on a wooden toolbox. Shoving away the temptation to let someone else make the decision, she pointed. "Randy, you can stack them against the work bench over there."

The room disintegrated into a whirl of greetings and activity. Once Holly got over the shock of being in charge, she realized it was no different from working at the front desk of the school, handling four different people's requests at the same time as she answered the phone and typed the principal's memos.

Robbie, Paul, and two of the cops took on fixing the nativity stable out in the field. Tim headed up the indoor carpentry unit, repairing damage to the figures themselves. Julia and the girls drew up the list of painting supplies, called it in to the hardware store, and took delivery.

The crew kept growing as local people got off work and showed up to help. Word had gotten around, probably through Tim's secretary Estelle Wilson, a former grade school teacher who had taught just about everyone in town. Holly was having a hard time finding enough space for everyone in the shed, so she went in search of Grady to ask permission to spread out into the barn.

He wasn't anywhere in the barn, so she crunched across the gravel of the road toward the house, pulling her coat tightly around her against the snow-chilled darkness. A single dim light burned in a window toward the back of the house. She walked up a set of creaky wooden steps and rapped on the side door. Rubbing her hands up and down her arms, she shivered and stamped her feet. The bulb overhead glimmered on and the door swung open.

The dim light pooled on the lenses of Grady's glasses as he said, "Yes?"

"I'm sorry to bother you," she said. "We've got more help than we expected, so I wondered if we could spread out into the barn. I don't want to disturb the animals."

"I reckon they'd welcome the company," the old man said. "None of 'em's skittish."

Holly caught the blue flicker of a television screen in a room beyond the farmer. She thought he would welcome some company too. "I was hoping you might help us out with some questions about the, um, clothing on the three kings. They're pretty badly crushed and it's hard to tell what their robes looked like."

"You make 'em look however you want," Grady said.

"Well, okay." Holly tried to think of some way to lure the man away from his lonely television viewing. "But we want to honor Bess's artistic vision of the scene." She'd heard Julia say something like that about some other artist's work.

"That's kind-thinking of you, but Bess just copied them out of a how-to magazine." The farmer started to turn away.

"My daughters would like you to see what they've done," Holly said, searching for the right leverage to pry him out of his too-quiet house.

He sighed. "I'll take a look then." He reached for the plaid jacket hanging on a hook beside the door.

She practically skipped along beside him because she was so pleased with herself for levering him out of his house. She could smell the loneliness on him. It wasn't right for anyone to be so isolated at Christmastime.

"I think you'll like how they've painted the hay around Baby Jesus," she said. "Julia showed them how to add some texture to the paint."

"She's that famous horse painter, ain't she?" Grady asked, plodding at her side. "Does the scary black stallions."

"That's right. She's here working on your nativity scene."

"Well, that's really something." Grady's voice picked up a bit with surprise.

They walked inside where light and noise spilled out of the shed's doorway into the quiet dark barn interior like one of Julia's slashing brushstrokes. Grady stopped. Holly tucked her hand around his elbow, the thick wool of his jacket rough against her palm, and tugged him gently forward beside her.

"Hi, Mr. Boone." Kayleigh raced up as they walked through the door. "Did you come to say thank you to everyone who's helping fix your nativity scene?"

Holly still had her hand on the farmer's arm, and she felt him stiffen, so she redirected the conversation. "No, I brought Mr. Boone to see how you painted the straw around Baby Jesus."

Kayleigh nodded and led the way to the newly painted manger. "Ms. Castillo showed us how to make the paint thicker in some places than others so it almost looks like real straw." She glanced up at the farmer. "I hope it's okay. We didn't change any of the colors. Ms. Castillo said we shouldn't."

Holly had released her hold on Grady's elbow, but she saw his Adam's apple bob up and down as he swallowed. "It looks fine," he said.

A look of relief crossed the old farmer's face as Robbie walked up, pulling off his work gloves and unzipping his jacket. "So did Holly get us permission to move out into the barn?" he asked. "It's getting a mite cold and dark outside and, as you can see, we've got a lot of helpers in here. Your nativity scene is considered a town treasure."

"I guess so." Grady swiveled his head to take in the crowd of volunteers crammed into the shed. As his glance touched on people's faces, they gave him a smile or a nod and a wave before going back to their tasks. "Well, I better get back to my knit—er, TV show. Use as much of the barn as you need."

Before Holly could stop him, Grady bolted for the door.

Holly sighed as she watched him disappear into the gloom of the barn. "He seemed so lonely, and I thought he'd be pleased to see how much everyone cares about his nativity scene."

Robbie touched the back of her hand. The heat of his fingertips seemed to soak all the way into her bones. "He *was* pleased. I could see it when he looked around. He just didn't know what to do with the feeling."

"Paul and I are going to bring the stable frame inside to work on now that it's dark." Robbie lowered his voice so only she could hear it. "You've done a fine thing here, Holly."

A feeling she couldn't quite name bloomed inside her. It was warm and bright, and it made her feel like she could take on the world.

Brianna approached them. "Mama? Can you help me get the lid off the purple paint can?"

Robbie stepped back with a nod.

As Holly followed her daughter to the workbench, she glanced back over her shoulder to find Robbie standing stock still in the midst of the activity, his blue gaze locked on her. She had that familiar sensation of everything fading away so that it was only the two of them. But this time she didn't feel a gentle warmth or a light flirtatious attraction. Now intense heat blasted through her, spiraling and coiling deep inside her belly until she nearly panted with the yearning to touch and be touched.

She whipped her head forward again.

She still wasn't strong enough to let another man have that kind of power over her.

CHAPTER FIVE

"Hello, hello! Look what I've brought." Claire's voice rang out and Holly turned to see her sister walk in, carrying a cooler. Tim followed behind her with two huge boxes stacked in his arms. "Food from The Aerie!"

Cheering erupted from the hungry workers, and the workbench was cleared in record time to hold the gourmet feast. As Claire and Holly set out the platters of crunchy fried chicken, truffle-infused French fries, and creamy spiced coleslaw, along with cornbread muffins and apple turnovers, Claire said, "What happened to my shy, retiring little sister? You've mobilized a whole battalion here."

Holly shook her head. "I just mentioned what happened to a couple of people, and they all showed up. It wasn't any great skill on my part."

Claire put down a pile of napkins and gave her sister a hug. "You made people care because you did, Holl. That's an amazing talent. And Tim tells me you're running the show. Go, little sis!"

Robbie's friend Pete snagged a plate while he surveyed the spread. "I shouldn't say it but sometimes I'm grateful to that bear that attacked Adam Bosch's dog. If Dr. Tim hadn't saved the dog's life, we wouldn't be eating gourmet take-out from a restaurant where you can't even get a reservation for the next two years."

Claire nodded. "Now that Trace is okay, you're allowed to say it, but not in Adam's hearing." She sighed. "I wish Adam would come down off his mountain along with his food. I worry about that man up there all alone."

"He's not exactly alone, seeing as folks use helicopters to get to his restaurant every night," Pete said.

Holly thought of the sense of isolation she'd felt when she'd been married to Frank. She could be in the midst of a flock of girlfriends or at the family Thanksgiving dinner and still feel she didn't have a friend in the world. "Just being around a lot of people doesn't keep you from being lonely."

Claire gave her shoulder a squeeze, and Holly felt tears burn behind her eyelids. "I'm going to take some food to the guys working on the stable." She grabbed a platter and randomly piled an assortment of food on it.

Her sister handed her some paper plates as she murmured, "I can't decide if Robbie looks better in his uniform or in a pair of tight jeans."

"You're a married woman." Holly gave her sister

an elbow in the ribs as she passed her. "But I can't decide either."

Holly stepped out of the brightly lit workshop into the near darkness of the barn. The stable repair crew had set up temporary lights at the far end, so she headed in that direction. Only Robbie and Paul were still working there, and she slowed her pace to admire the two men bathed in the brilliant floodlight. Robbie's hair was gilded nearly blond while Paul's dark head picked up auburn glints. Paul was whipcord lean, while Robbie retained the defined muscles he'd developed as an athlete.

Robbie had shed his jacket and rolled up his shirtsleeves so she could see the line of tendon and muscle flex in his forearms as he hammered the supports together. The pull of his shirt fabric across his quarterback's shoulders fanned the flicker of heat deep in her gut into a full-on flame.

She came to a halt in the shadows as she fought against the intensity of her reaction to Robbie. She needed to get a grip on herself before she tried to carry on a normal conversation with the man who made her want to run her hands over every inch of his skin.

As she paused, Robbie stopped hammering to wipe his forehead with the back of his hand. Paul spoke into the sudden silence. "John LeGrande called to say he owes me a favor. Which is interesting since I thought I owed him one. That must have been one hell of an interview you gave them."

Robbie shrugged.

Paul leaned against one of the barn's wooden support columns and gestured toward the half-repaired stable. "You know you won't find this in Atlanta. Folks are nice enough down there, but they don't fix each other's nativity scenes."

Robbie flipped his hammer end over end and caught it again. "I'm willing to take that trade-off. LeGrande says I can make detective in ten months."

Robbie was leaving Sanctuary. It felt as though her bones were dissolving, making her knees rubbery, as the knowledge seared through her.

"Ten months from when?" Paul asked.

"I start February first. That's when they have the budget for the new position." Robbie reached out to shake Paul's hand. "Thanks for putting me in touch with the right people, and for the recommendation."

He began to pivot in her direction, so she forced the wobbling corners of her mouth into a false smile and gripped the edges of the platter so hard her knuckles went white. "Hey, you working men," she squeaked, "I brought some fuel for your muscles." She lifted the tray to chest height in hopes the food would distract them from her lack of composure.

"Lady, you are a sight for sore eyes." Paul strode forward to take the platter from her.

She wasn't looking at him, though. Her attention was on Robbie, who was scanning her face as though she were a witness whose honesty he was weighing. He must be trying to decide whether she'd heard the conversation and might spill his secret to the rest of the town. She kept her mockery of a smile in place as she thrust the paper plates in Robbie's general direction. "You've got a lot to get done in a short time, so I won't stay here and bother you."

She spun on her heel and somehow managed to reel back to the workshop. Stepping inside the door, she tried to bring her focus to the project at hand, but her thoughts kept circling back to Robbie's unwitting revelation. She stood with her arms crossed, rubbing her hands up and down her biceps as she shivered and wondered why his upcoming departure was hitting her so hard.

Claire appeared at her side. "Holly, you look like you've seen a ghost. What's going on?"

It took a moment for Holly to focus on her sister's words. Once she did, all she could manage was to shake her head.

"Come on." Claire took her wrist and towed her toward the shed's outdoor exit. "We'll sit in my car to keep warm."

Claire hustled her along the edge of the farm road to where her SUV was parked. Holly climbed in the passenger seat and tried to pull herself together as Claire punched the heat on full blast.

"It's none of my business really," Holly said when Claire swiveled sideways in her seat with that *tell me everything, sister* look. "I just overheard something I shouldn't have and it gave me a bit of a shock."

"Well, it becomes *my* business when it upsets my sister." Claire flicked her long, dark ponytail over her shoulder. "Is it about Robbie?"

Holly realized the awkward position she was in, knowing a secret she shouldn't. She nodded. "But I can't tell you what I heard. It's not public knowledge."

Her sister gave her a serene smile and waited. Claire had helped her take back her life after Frank abused her and stole all her money. Holly owed her the truth. She fidgeted with the zipper on her sweatshirt. "Robbie's taking a job in Atlanta. It starts February first." A cry of denial tried to wrench itself from her throat. "Claire, I didn't know how much I'd hoped for something with him until I found out he's leaving."

Her sister took Holly's fidgety hands in her own. "I know you're grateful to him for protecting you from Frank."

"It's not gratitude when you want to rip his clothes off."

"Oh." Claire released her hands and leaned back against the car door. "That kind of something."

Holly dropped her hands in her lap and stared down at them. "It's not like we've ever even had a date, so it's ridiculous for me to feel this way."

"You can't stop yourself from *feeling*. What you have to figure out is whether to act on it or not."

"Of course I'm not going to act on it," Holly said, jerking her gaze to her sister. "I'm not ready."

"For what?"

"To give a man a say in my life," Holly said. "I need to figure out how to be on my own first. To show Brianna and Kayleigh how to live as an independent woman."

Claire gave her a quizzical look. "I thought you wanted to get him naked, not hand over your life decisions to him."

"I, but——." She'd never even considered just having a physical relationship with Robbie. He seemed like too honorable a guy for that kind of fling.

"I'm not telling you how to live your life," Claire said, "but everyone can feel the sizzle between you two."

"They can?" Holly shook her head. "I don't feel very sizzling since Frank."

"I know that creep did a number on your self-confidence, but I've seen lots of men get a gleam in their eye when they look at you."

Tears threatened. Frank had cheated on her when he traveled for his job. When she found out, he told her it was her fault for being so boring in the bedroom. Robbie might think she was pretty, she didn't trust her ability to hold his interest in that way. She couldn't admit that though, even to Claire. "But what kind of example is that for my daughters?"

Claire sighed. "You are the best mother in the world, but even the most perfect mothers need to have some grown-up fun or they will set a very bad example for their children by losing their minds. You just have to be discreet. And I'll help you."

"What do you mean?" Holly had a vision of Claire guarding the bedroom door as she and Robbie climbed under the covers.

"I'll babysit. The girls can come over to spend the night with me." Claire thought for a moment. "This Saturday."

"But it's only five days from now and I don't know what Robbie's plans are for Saturday. He may already have a date."

"So find out and get back to me."

"But I can't ask *him* out. I mean, he's a man."

Claire gave her a look. "What century are you living in?" Then she relented. "Offer to cook him dinner as a thank you for fixing the manger scene."

"But a dozen people helped."

"It's just a ploy. He'll get the message."

The car's heat felt scorching, so Holly unzipped her sweatshirt. Did she want Robbie to get the message? What if he had no interest in her that way? What if it ruined the friendship between them? "It seems risky."

"Sweetie, you lived with an abusive husband. *That's* risky." Claire's expression softened. "I just want to see you happy again."

"But I am happy. My children are the joy of my life. Thanks to you, I own my house. I have a steady job and plenty of friends."

Claire shook her head. "You need someone to love you so much, he will put you first in his life."

"Well, that won't be Robbie, because he's leaving."

Claire looked out into the darkness, her mouth set in a grim line. "I was once where you are. I couldn't imagine ever making myself vulnerable to a man again, but I met Tim. And my whisper horse Willow showed me how to trust, even after you've been hurt." Claire brought her gaze back to her sister. "Think about it, Holly. You don't want to spend the rest of your life wondering what you might have missed."

CHAPTER SIX

Holly surveyed the arrangement of the refurbished manger scene on its outdoor hill. A crew of cops had brought everything down in a pickup truck, set up the stable structure, and left Holly, Robbie, and Julia to arrange the figures. "What do you think, Julia? Should Mary be a little farther to the right?"

The artist tilted her head, debating. "Maybe if you shift the shepherd left and Joseph farther forward..."

With a dramatic groan, Robbie picked up the shepherd he'd just placed and moved it a foot to the left.

Julia shook her head. "No, it's better where it was."

Robbie narrowed his eyes at the two women, but one corner of his mouth twitched upward. "Are you messing with me?"

"Maybe," Holly said.

"It's just that you look so good in that uniform of yours," Julia said. "We want to enjoy the view a little longer."

Holly could feel the heat in her cheeks as Robbie put down the wooden figure in its original location with a huff of a laugh. Brianna and Kayleigh had stayed in the barn to see Noël, which meant Julia's well-known frankness had no constraints. Of course, Holly had been thinking something along those same lines.

Robbie picked up a sledgehammer and pounded the stakes into the ground to hold the shepherd in place. The power of his muscles and the torque of his body drew her eye like a magpie to a sparkly button, and sent a shudder of pure longing through her body.

She wished she had the nerve to follow Claire's advice. But despite the show of strength she put on for Brianna and Kayleigh, she still felt as though she were made of glass as thin as her Christmas tree ornaments. If Robbie rejected her, she was afraid she would shatter into razor-edged shards that were impossible to put back together.

He finished sinking the last stake and slung the hammer over his shoulder while he checked the stability of the shepherd.

"He'd make a great model for Thor," Julia murmured, as he sauntered toward them, his stride fluid and assured. He seemed neither self-conscious about nor flattered by Julia's appraisal, which made Holly happy.

"What's the verdict?" he asked, coming up beside Holly and turning to take in the nativity scene. Before Holly could answer, he gave an admiring whistle. "No need to ask. It looks better than it ever did before."

"The fresh paint makes it brighter," Holly agreed, warmed by an inner glow at his praise. "And we moved a couple of the figures to different spots. I hope Grady won't mind that."

Robbie shook his head. "Grady will be grateful you've given him back Bess's pet project."

Restoring the manger scene had set back Holly's own Christmas preparations by two days, but when she looked at the vividly robed figures gathered around the new baby on his bed of straw, she was certain it had been worth it. Like all great traditions, this nativity scene brought the folks of Sanctuary together, weaving shared bonds of community around the hearts of people from all walks of life.

"Grady and the girls should see this," Robbie said.

"I've got to get back to my studio," Julia said. "I have a show coming up and I'm behind."

"I didn't mean to take you away from your work," Holly said with a flash of guilt.

Julia waved away Holly's concern with a grin. "I'm always behind. Just ask your sister."

"Thank you!" Holly called as Julia headed off toward the motorcycle she'd roared up on earlier. Turning to Robbie, she stuck her hands in her pockets and scuffed at the snow. "You probably need to go too."

"No, I'm good." His voice held something that made Holly look up at his face. The color of his eyes seemed more intense than usual, and a sharpness around his jaw suggested he was holding himself in check in some way. She thought his gaze dropped to her lips, but then he gave her a friendly smile, and she decided she had imagined the whole thing. "Let's head up to the barn. It's tough going through the snow so I'll give you some help." He extended his gloved hand to her.

She pulled her hand out of her pocket and put it in his, watching as his fingers closed around hers and feeling the strength of his grip down to her bones. They crunched across the snowy field side by side, their breath coming out in puffy little clouds. The sun was dropping behind the mountains, washing the snow with pink.

She kept her gaze on the gate, but in her peripheral vision, she could see Robbie's long, athletic stride. The power he radiated made her feel safe, even as it sent ripples of excitement shimmering over her skin.

It was a moment she wanted to stitch into her memory so she could take it out and snuggle into it after he was gone.

Claire's words floated back to nag at her. Would this moment be enough or would she regret not trying for more?

She opened her mouth, but no words formed, so she closed it again.

As they reached the gate, Robbie tossed the hammer over the fence post before he stepped in front of her, taking hold of her other hand as well. She swore she felt the heat of his gaze as he scanned her face. She tilted her head up toward him in a subtle invitation, but all he said was, "I know you don't want to hear it, but you saved something important to the whole town."

She waited, willing him to give her some signal that he admired more than just her civic spirit. She might have even swayed toward him just a bit with her lips slightly parted.

He squeezed both her hands and released her to swing open the gate.

She shoved her hands into her pockets and stomped up the road before he could latch the gate behind them.

Darn the man for refusing to give her any help at all!

"Mama, can we take Noël down to the nativity scene?" Brianna asked. "She's going to be in it so she should get to see it." She and Kayleigh stood on a hay bale just outside Noël's stall, petting the donkey's neck and head.

"You just want to spend more time with that donkey," Holly said, parking her hands on her hips. The donkey's eyes were closed, and she could swear the creature wore an expression of total bliss.

Brianna nodded. "She's really sweet. She would never bite anyone." She shifted her gaze to the man standing beside Holly. "Isn't that right, Captain Robbie?"

"Well, she's never bitten me," Robbie said, "but animals can be unpredictable."

Brianna was far too perceptive, and Robbie was being too kind. Holly was *not* going to look like a coward in front of them. She unlatched the stall door and walked in, stretching out her arm to pat the donkey's neck. Noël's fuzzy coat was soft and springy. The donkey turned to look at her, so she yanked back her hand and took a quick step away. She nearly collided with Brianna and Kayleigh, who had seized the opportunity to follow her into the stall.

"Can we take her with us, Mama?" Kayleigh chimed in, opening her eyes wide in her best pleading look.

"It's pretty hard to refuse those two," Robbie said, his expression one of appreciation as he joined the crowd around Noël.

"You're not helping." Holly slanted a wry look at him before turning back to her children. "We can't take Noël out of the stall without Grady's permission, so I'll have to go ask him."

"He should come see the nativity scene too," Brianna pointed out.

Holly nodded and turned to leave the stall. The donkey suddenly swung her rear end around, banging into Holly so she was knocked full-length against Robbie.

"Oof!" she gasped, as her body and his collided. His arms came up around her when she grabbed at his jacket for balance. It was like being surrounded by a warm, breathing oak. She felt desire rip through her as her breasts were crushed against his chest and their thighs slammed into contact.

She hadn't been in a man's arms since Frank left, but she hadn't felt the loss until now. A great yearning swirled in her belly and she glanced up to read Robbie's reaction. As she met his gaze, she felt his arms tighten around her. She expected him to smile or toss off a joke, but he just stared down at her.

"What on earth got into that donkey?" Holly said, pressing her weight backwards to break his hold. For a long moment, his grip didn't loosen.

Finally, his lips tipped up into a smile that seemed strained and he released her. "Guess she thought her stall was getting too crowded. I'll go rustle up a lead line." He was out the stall door before Holly could thank him for catching her.

Holly rubbed her hands on her thighs, as she tried to decipher her reaction and his.

"Are you okay, Mama?" Kayleigh asked.

"Noël didn't mean to hurt you," Brianna said.

"I know that, sweetie." She yanked her thoughts back to the children. "I'm fine."

A lie. She was reeling from feeling Robbie's hard, male body against hers. Their stroll across the snowy field had been something out of a sweet romantic comedy. The way she felt now was dark and primitive and so potent she could barely think straight.

"Let me go talk to Mr. Boone," she said.

When she walked out of the barn door, the winter air smacked into her like cold, hard reality, blowing away the sensual haze she'd been wrapped in. It was better this way.

She knocked on the side door of the house again and waited. She knew Grady was there because they'd checked in with him before they'd started setting up the nativity scene. It took a long moment before she heard footsteps and the door opened.

"Evening." The light behind the old farmer cast a gleam on his bald head and glowed on the yellow stripes in the plaid of his shirt.

"We finished the nativity scene, and we thought you'd like to come see it," Holly said.

Grady seemed taken aback. "Does it look any different?"

Holly had to be honest. "It has fresh paint, and we shifted a couple of figures."

"I reckon I'll see it tonight when I put the animals out," Grady said.

Holly felt a little thud of disappointment. "Well, okay." She shoved her hands into her pockets. "Would it be all right if we took Noël down to see the scene? The girls thought she—" It sounded ridiculous to say the donkey would want to see the place where she'd be on display. "She might like the exercise."

A cloud of guilt passed over Grady's face. "The little girls are going to see it?"

Holly nodded.

"Well, since they worked on it, I guess I should go take a gander." He turned away from the door. "Come inside while I get my boots on."

She stepped onto the cracked green linoleum of the mud room as the old farmer plunked down on a bench and pulled off his slippers. Lying on top of a small chest of drawers by the kitchen door was a partly completed baby blanket still on the knitting needles. It looked as though his wife had laid it down there before she died, and Grady hadn't been able to throw it away or even move it. Holly's chest tightened with sadness as she reached out to brush her fingers over the soft stripes of mint green and pale yellow.

She caught Grady watching her and pulled her hand back. A deep blush climbed his cheeks as he bent over to yank on his rubber Wellington boots. "I make 'em for that Project Linus," he said gruffly. "For babies in the hospital."

"*You* made it? I thought—" Holly stopped herself. "It's beautiful."

Grady pushed up from the bench and reached for his jacket. "Bess taught me how to knit when she got sick because she'd promised six blankets and had only finished four."

Holly tried to picture Grady, in his flannel shirt and rubber boots, going to the yarn store and choosing the skin-caressing yarn in baby-appropriate colors. "It's wonderful of you to carry on her work," she said, thinking how very little anyone knows about the private lives of the people around them. Everyone had thought she and Frank had a wonderful marriage. Only Claire had been able to see behind the façade, and that was because she had insisted on helping Holly daily when she had been so ill with Lyme disease.

Grady shrugged and held the door open for Holly. "It makes watching the television less of a time waste."

As they started across the road toward the barn, Holly tucked her hand around his elbow. "You know, Grady, I think you're just pretending to be a curmudgeon."

The old farmer didn't say anything, but he bent his arm so her hand rested there more comfortably.

Robbie felt a ping of jealousy when Holly walked into the barn escorted by Grady Boone, smiling as though she and the old farmer had just shared a private joke. It took him back to the walk across the field with Holly. He'd wanted that field to go on for miles, with her tramping along beside him so close he could hear the intake of her breath as the cold made her gasp slightly. He could feel the shape of her hand in his and watch the way the setting sun brushed its light over her cheeks and dark hair.

But that was nothing compared to the lust that had walloped him when that blasted donkey had shoved her soft, warm body right up against him. Once he got his arms around her, he had to fight the temptation to pull her down in the straw, cradling her body over his while he tasted those soft lips he dreamt about in ways that forced him to take a cold shower in the morning.

Nope. Not going there.

He shook his head and unlatched Noël's stall door, letting Brianna lead the donkey out since he was sure Grady would agree to anything Holly asked. She had that effect on people; she was so sweet and generous, she made the folks around her behave better to match up.

"Grady, I see you've fallen prey to the charms of the Snedegar girls," Robbie said as the farmer bent down to receive a hug from Kayleigh.

The older man hesitated a moment and then put one arm around the more reserved Brianna's shoulders and gave her a squeeze. He produced a rusty smile when Holly beamed her approval at him. Grady turned to Robbie. "You hang around them a lot yourself."

Robbie choked on a laugh. Who'd have thought old Grady had it in him to give as good as he got? "I'm a sucker for a pretty face, and when there are three of them, I'm sunk."

Kayleigh did a little twirl at the compliment.

"Careful," Brianna said to her sister, "You don't

want to scare Noël."

"Noël's steady as a redwood in a windstorm." Grady rested his hand on the donkey's back as Brianna led her out the barn door and onto the road.

Except when Holly was standing beside him in Noël's stall.

"Captain Robbie, my friend Teresa's mama says you're a lady killer." Kayleigh inserted herself between Robbie and Holly and took their hands. "But that doesn't sound very nice."

He heard a choked giggle from Holly and had to quell a grin of relief. "That's what you call a figure of speech, sweetheart," he said to the little girl. "I don't kill ladies. Or anyone else."

"But you have a gun."

"That's to keep bad guys from killing me," Robbie said.

"So what did her mama mean?"

"She's like a dog with a bone," Holly said, her brown eyes dancing at Robbie's predicament.

"She meant the ladies like me," Robbie said, keeping it simple.

"Well, I already knew that," Kayleigh scoffed. "You're the police captain. You keep ladies safe."

He saw the shadow that fell over Holly's face and knew she was remembering what had happened with her rat bastard of an ex-husband. Robbie was aware that it embarrassed her to know he had witnessed the ugliness, but the truth was he felt guilty for not realizing what was going on sooner. Someday maybe he'd meet Snedegar in a dark alley and see how the scumbag liked having the tables turned on him. Not that he planned to travel to Mexico to track the man down. He felt it was good riddance to bad rubbish. But there was always a chance the dirtball would come back.

And he planned to be ready.

Kayleigh dropped their hands and skipped ahead to chat with the farmer.

"No, I'm not telling you who Teresa's mom is," Holly said with a laugh in her voice.

"I could figure it out in about thirty seconds," Robbie said. "I know every family in Sanctuary."

"You don't sound especially happy about that," she said.

She saw too much. "It's a small town," he said, keeping his voice neutral. He glanced sideways to find her scanning his face as though she were debating something. For a long moment he found himself unable to look away as her lips parted. His pace slowed.

The thump of helicopter rotors broke through the heat building between them, and he dragged his gaze upward to focus on the chopper beating its way to the mountaintop helipad of The Aerie. It was a high end Sikorsky, one he'd love to get his hands on the controls of. He'd run through every kind of flying machine parked at the local airport, including the Bell helicopter, in his efforts to escape the confines of Sanctuary for a few hours. He was looking for a new challenge, and this baby would offer that in spades.

Would he still seek the wide open skies once he got to Atlanta? Or would the other challenges it offered be enough?

Hell if he knew.

Holly saw the longing on Robbie's face as he narrowed his eyes to track the helicopter across the darkening sky. It was a big sleek machine with red and white lights glistening against its shiny blue paint. She followed it too, trying to imagine what it would be like to ride in an aircraft as casually as you would a car. The highest she'd ever been off the ground was the top of the double Ferris wheel at the West Virginia State Fair.

That was it!

She came to a halt, knowing Robbie would too. As the helicopter disappeared around the mountain, he brought his gaze back to her. She waited until Grady and the girls were rattling the latch of the gate before she spoke. "Will you take me flying?"

She held her breath. He didn't answer immediately, and she felt the knot of nerves in her chest wind tighter as she hurried to fill the awkward silence. "I've never been up in a plane and I'd like to go—" She slammed her mouth shut.

She'd been about to say, "Before you leave."

He was waiting for her to finish, but all she could do was wave her hand in a vague way.

"Sure thing," he said. "I'll take the girls too."

"No! Only me!" She blurted before he could call out to them. "I want to see what it's like before I take them up."

"I'm an experienced pilot." Robbie sounded as though he might be insulted.

She shook her head. "It's not that. If we take them, I'll be watching their reactions. I want to experience it on my own first." And with him.

The slight scowl drawing his brows together vanished, as excitement made his eyes seem to ignite. "I'd be honored to show you the sky."

CHAPTER SEVEN

Holly put down the dinner plate she was rinsing as Claire walked in the door, bringing with her a waft of frigid night air. "You're front page news, little sister," she said, waving the local weekly newspaper at Holly.

"What are you talking about, big sister?" Holly asked, taking the paper.

"Aunt Claire!" Kayleigh jumped out of the chair at the kitchen table where she was decorating a Christmas ornament. "Your dress is so pretty. I like the pink color."

"I know it's your favorite." Claire kissed both her nieces. "Did your mama tell you about our sleepover on Saturday?"

"Yes, ma'am. But today's only Thursday, so we have to wait a long time." Kayleigh spun around with all the pent-up anticipation.

Claire laughed as Holly unfolded the *Sanctuary Sentinel* to find a photograph of the restored nativity scene. Grady was posed with his hand resting on the figure of Joseph, looking like a deer in headlights. "Poor man," Holly breathed.

"May I see too, Mama?" Brianna peered over Holly's arm.

She lowered the paper so her daughter could see it. "Just remember Mrs. Weikle likes to make things sound more dramatic than they really are," she warned as she read the screaming headline: "Sacred Sanctuary tradition saved by school secretary."

The rest of the article stuck mostly to the facts, although Bernie Weikle's description of the torn and mangled wooden figures sounded more like a murder scene than some smashed-up pieces of plywood.

"Gosh, Mama, she says without you, the 'sacred and cherished tradition would have been lost forever.' She says you're the 'hero of the day'," Brianna quoted, lifting shining eyes to her mother.

"And she's right," Claire said. She came over and wrapped her arms around Holly in a tight hug before pulling back to look her sister in the eye.

"You're going to give me a swelled head." Holly still didn't feel like she'd done anything out of the ordinary. However, she thought she could use the occasion as a lesson for her children. She turned back to her girls. "Just remember how many people were there in the barn working with us. They took time out of their busy days when we needed them. When you need help, you should never hesitate to ask for it. That's what Sanctuary is all about."

It was a lesson she'd learned the hard way.

"Will you help me glue the sequins on my ornament?" Kayleigh smiled up at her aunt.

Claire laughed and slanted a look at her sister. "Sure," she said, pulling out a chair. "It looks like fun."

Once the ornaments were finished and the girls were in bed, Holly poured two glasses of wine and dragged Claire into her bedroom, closing and locking the door. "It was a bad idea to ask Robbie to take me flying. I should have just invited him over for dinner and left it at that," she said, pacing across the floor while Claire stacked up the pillows, slipped off her boots, and settled herself on the bed.

Claire took a leisurely sip of wine. "Why?"

Holly stopped to stare at her sister. "Because I've never been in an airplane before."

"You'll be with Robbie. You trust him, don't you?"

"He's an experienced pilot." Holly repeated his words with a slight smile. "But that doesn't mean I won't be nervous about being up so high. I cried on the chair lift when we went skiing at Snowshoe."

"You were ten. And an airplane is enclosed."

Holly took a swig of wine and started pacing again. "Robbie's seen me being pathetic once. I don't want it to happen again."

"You were not pathetic. You were the victim of domestic violence." Claire's tone was harsh, but Holly knew her anger was directed at Frank.

Holly still felt shame at the fact that she'd stayed

with her abusive ex-husband for so long. Even though Claire told her over and over again it wasn't her fault, she didn't believe that in her heart.

Claire must have seen something in her face, because her voice softened. "Holl, you know that being brave doesn't mean not being scared, right? Courage is refusing to let fear control your actions. And you have more courage than anyone I know."

"And you're the world's best sister," Holly said, wanting to change the subject that had somehow strayed away from her immediate concern.

"That is very true and I can prove it." Claire set her wineglass on the bedside table and reached down to pick up the shiny green shopping bag she'd carried in with her. It was embossed with name of an exclusive shop at the Laurels, the nearby resort hotel. "Look at what I brought you."

Holly slid her glass onto the table and sat down on the bed beside Claire. The bag was stuffed with gold tissue paper. She pulled it out and two wisps of deep red lace floated onto the quilt. When Holly picked them up, they unfolded themselves into a sheer bra and tiny bikini panties.

"Those are for Saturday," Claire said. "Wear a white blouse."

"I can't do that." Holly held the filmy garment up to her chest. "The red lace would show through."

Claire's lips curved into a sly smile.

"Oh!" Holly gasped as she caught her sister's expression. She picked up the panties. "I refuse to wear a white skirt though!"

"It's winter, so that wouldn't be appropriate," Claire agreed.

"Do you wear this kind of thing all the time?" Holly put her hand under the lace to see how transparent it was.

"Only when I'm hoping for a certain reaction from Tim. And then I don't wear it for long." Claire got up and headed for Holly's closet. "Now let's see what Robbie is going to peel off you to get to the red lace."

Sheer panic closed up Holly's throat at the realization that all this was supposed to end with her and Robbie in bed together. "I can't...I don't...oh, Claire!"

Her sister backed out of the closet with a look of concern on her face. "What is it, sweetie?" She sat on the bed and wrapped her arm around Holly's shoulders.

"It's been a long time since..." Holly waved her hand vaguely.

"Since you had sex?"

Holly nodded.

"It's like riding a bicycle. You never forget how," Claire said.

Holly felt her sister's grip relax. "It's more than that. It was only Frank for so many years."

"I'm sure Robbie will be better than Frank."

"But what if *I'm* not any good?" Holly finally managed to force out.

"Oh, sweetie, why would you worry about that?"

Holly stared down at the lace she'd crumpled

into a ball between her hands. "That's why Frank cheated on me," she whispered.

Claire's arm went rigid across her back. "No, it's not," she said, fury in her voice again. "He cheated on you because he was a self-centered, lying, immoral pig. It had nothing to do with anything you did or didn't do." She softened her voice. "You are a beautiful, sexy woman. When Robbie sees that red lace peeking through your white blouse, he's going to have a hard time keeping his mind on piloting the plane."

"Way to make me less nervous about flying." Holly buried her face in Claire's shoulder and said in a muffled voice, "I hope you're right."

They stayed like that for a long moment. "Okay, back to clothing selection," Claire said, sitting back and reaching for Holly's wineglass. She put it in her sister's hand and headed back for the closet. "Now let's put together an ensemble that says 'keep your hands on the controls of the plane, but rip off my clothes after we land'."

CHAPTER EIGHT

"You've gotten quiet," Robbie said as he swung his SUV into a parking space in front of Sanctuary International Airport's single terminal on Saturday afternoon. The low brick building sprawled across what had once been a pasture. Now the chain-link fence extending from the terminal surrounded a flock of parked aircraft rather than a herd of grazing cows.

Holly had been hoping for a snowstorm, but the day had dawned clear, the air made crystalline by the winter cold. She rubbed her palms on the wool of the red skirt Claire had loaned her. Her sister had convinced her that the skirt paired with high-heeled black leather boots was the perfect outfit for flying. Claire had even talked her into wearing the red bra under a cream silk blouse, but Holly had made sure her winter coat was already on and buttoned when Robbie picked her up. "I'm nervous about being up so high."

Robbie shifted his gaze away from the planes lined up on the tarmac, turning those vivid blue eyes in her direction. "How about I give you a tour of the airport and the planes? Then you can decide if you want to go up."

His understanding almost undermined the courage she'd been shoring up all week. She took in a deep breath, catching a whiff of the citrus-scented soap he'd used that morning. She'd never before been this close to him when they were alone. Her nerve endings began to hum with awareness and anticipation. "I want to go up," she said, hoping to talk herself into believing it.

He smiled, his teeth white and even. She caught a hint of a dimple in his right cheek. "You'll be glad you did." He glanced back at the planes. "Everything looks different from up there."

Holly forced herself to smile as she unbuckled her seat belt. Robbie was out of his seat and coming around to hold the door for her before she had gathered up her handbag and climbed out of the car.

White Christmas lilted from the loudspeaker as he pushed open the terminal door for her. "Let me pick up the keys from Crystal," he said, leading the way down a linoleum tile-floored corridor lined with office doors. The walls were bright with cardboard Santas, festoons of green and red tinsel, and wreaths made of shiny gold Christmas tree balls.

Robbie stopped in front of an open door and gestured Holly inside. Behind a metal desk, a woman with brown hair cut man-short spun her chair away from a computer screen. She was extraordinarily beautiful, but Holly was prepared for that. Crystal Detch had made a big splash as a model before she got her heart broken by some rich man in New York City. She'd come back to Sanctuary and taken over running the airport when her father retired from the job five years before. As far as Holly knew, Crystal had not been on a single date since her return.

"First time up, I hear," Crystal said to Holly as she plucked a key ring off the board beside her. "You'll get hooked." She handed the keys to Robbie. "The Cessna's all fueled and ready. I checked her over myself. Not that I want to stop you from doing your own preflight check."

Robbie tossed the keys up and caught them behind his back, making his brown leather jacket pull tight across his wide shoulders. "You know I will. Precious cargo." He gave Holly a sideways smile.

"The Cessna's a sweet craft," Crystal said. "A little old lady only flew it to church on Sundays."

Holly forced a nervous smile. Was her anxiety so obvious that Crystal was trying to reassure her too?

Robbie walked over to a row of clipboards hanging on the opposite wall, taking one down and flipping through several pages attached to it, his gaze intent. Holly must have looked puzzled because Crystal said, "It's the maintenance log for the plane. McGraw here is one of the smartest pilots I know. He never goes up in an aircraft he doesn't trust one hundred percent."

"Better safe than sorry at 15,000 feet." Robbie

rehung the clipboard. "Looks good. Let's go see her in person, Holly."

"Who does the plane really belong to?" Holly asked as they walked toward the outside door to the bouncing melody of *Rudolf the Red-Nosed Reindeer.*

"A guy who flies in to stay at his vacation home on the golf course at the Laurels," Robbie said. "He doesn't like the plane to sit around unused so he lets a few local pilots rent it when he's in residence."

He pushed the door open and ushered Holly out in front of him. Although the sun shone in the brilliant blue sky, a chilly breeze whipped across the open tarmac. It caught the end of Holly's scarf and flipped it into her face as she was slipping her gloves on. Robbie reached out to pull the scarf away and his fingertips brushed against her cheek. She glanced up to thank him and found his gaze riveted on her lips. Unable to stop the reflex, she licked them. A muscle in his jaw twitched and he looked away.

A mixture of confidence and a whole different kind of nervousness surged through her.

His jacket flapped open as he yanked on his gloves. The wind flattened his white shirt against his torso, revealing the definition of his muscled chest and abs. She was torn between appreciation and worry. His body was so perfect. After two pregnancies, hers wasn't.

"This way," he said, offering her the crook of his arm.

He kept up a running commentary on the various planes they passed, but Holly was focused on the feel of him against her side as she deliberately tucked herself in close. Sneaking glances up at him, she learned he had fine lines at the corners of his eyes and an inward curl at the corner of his mouth when he smiled. He must have shaved for her because there was barely a glint of a blond whisker on his cheeks or chin.

When Robbie said something about Santa Claus, it broke through her distracted haze of fascination. "Santa Claus?" she repeated, looking around to see they were standing in front of a bright red helicopter.

"I'm flying Ed Hardy to the regional hospital over at Broadmoor tomorrow to take the toys to the kids there."

Ed was a rotund man with a long white beard who was in great demand to play Santa Claus every holiday season. The rest of the year he ran Hardy's Hardware in downtown Sanctuary.

"I dropped off three boxes of new toys donated by the school staff for the toy drive," Holly said. "The kids are going to love them."

"Most of the donations went over in a truck today," Robbie said. "Ed has just enough to fill up his pack for when he arrives in the helicopter."

Holly eyed the helicopter and said a silent prayer of thanks that she didn't have to ride in the unwieldy-looking metal contraption crouched under its drooping rotors.

Robbie led her past the chopper to a gleaming white single propeller plane with black-and-gold stripes swooshing down its sides. It looked fast just sitting on the apron. "But this beauty is pure pleasure to fly. Her owner loaded her up with everything top-of-the-line."

He fitted a key into the lock and pushed the door upward.

"It looks just like the inside of a car," Holly said, amazed at the luxurious leather seats in a golden tan. "But where's the steering wheel?"

Robbie pointed to something that looked like a video game control stick, one on each side of the plane. There were video screens across the dashboard and between the seats, so she guessed that made sense. "She handles almost like a jet," he said.

He showed her where to step and wrapped his hands around her waist to boost her up with a power that made her feel almost weightless. She scrambled into the contoured seat as Robbie climbed up beside her. "I'm going to do a visual check on the exterior."

Holly nodded and he lowered the door, locking it down so firmly the plane rocked slightly. She took a deep breath and peered around the cabin. It seemed very small for something that was going to take them thousands of feet up into thin air. She wrapped her arms across her chest, telling herself it was the cold that was making her shiver.

A few minutes later, the other side of the plane dipped as the door opened, and Robbie dropped into the seat beside hers, giving her a grin and a thumbs-up before he closed his own door.

His smile lingered as he brought the engine to life and ran through a series of tests, flipping switches and scrolling through screens, explaining all the time what he was doing. She almost forgot her nerves in the pleasure of hearing his deep voice and watching his big, square hands move with such sureness through the tasks.

Lifting two sets of headphones from the storage console, he handed one to Holly. "The cabin is pretty sound-proofed but it's still easier to talk with these. And you can hear the tower and other airplanes."

He reached across Holly, his arm pressing lightly against her ribs, as he tested the security of her latch. "Good to go. Now buckle up."

She fumbled with the seatbelt, not sure how to arrange the straps. Robbie twisted in his seat and settled them into place. She sucked in her breath as his fingers just barely brushed against the side of her breast. Despite the thick wool fabric of her coat separating his skin from hers, she felt a jolt of arousal.

Between her anxiety about flying and Robbie's disturbing presence, Holly's nerves were wound tight. Her hands shook slightly as she fitted the headset over her ears and flipped down the microphone. It didn't help when Robbie's voice poured directly into her ear. "Crystal, this is Robbie McGraw. Pre-flight check complete and I'm ready to roll."

Crystal's voice came back with a string of

information involving wind and directions and numbers as well as permission to use the runway.

Robbie reeled off more jargon, and the plane started to move. Holly looked for something to hold onto but all she saw was the control stick on her side and that, she wasn't going to touch. So she hooked her thumbs in her coat pockets and tried to appear calm.

They taxied onto the runway and pivoted so the nose of the plane pointed down the straight stretch of tarmac that seemed to go on for miles. Out of the corner of her eye she saw Robbie's hands touching buttons and screens but she couldn't look away from the distant end of the runway. That was the point of no return. She would be in the air by then if she didn't beg Robbie to stop.

The engine sound rose to a roar and the plane shuddered with pent-up energy. She pulled her hands out of her pockets and clenched them around the seat belt straps.

"Holly? You good?" She dragged her gaze away from the runway to find Robbie looking at her with concern.

She nodded emphatically because she knew her voice would shake if she tried to speak.

"Here we go!" He did something with the joystick and the plane leapt forward.

She couldn't stifle a gasp but the engine noise covered it up.

The aircraft bounced along the tarmac for several seconds. Then the nose tilted up and the bumps ceased. Her muscles squeezed with anxiety as she realized they were airborne. She'd expected to have the whole length of the runway to get used to the idea of taking off.

The airplane suddenly surged upward and then dropped, leaving her stomach in her throat. Holly closed her eyes and whispered an incoherent prayer.

"It's a little gusty down near the ground. Probably the advance edge of the storm that's blowing in tonight." Robbie's voice was calm. "We'll get above it soon."

A dizzy sense of disorientation seized her as she felt the plane tilt. She opened her eyes to see the mountains slanting at a crazy angle as they turned and climbed at the same time. Every fiber of her body was screaming in panic, and she turned to ask Robbie to take her back to the solid, reliable earth.

One glance at his face and the words died in her throat. His eyes glowed with what she could only describe as sheer joy. He was leaning forward slightly as though he couldn't wait to see what was around the next mountain ridge. He looked alive in a way she hadn't seen in years, maybe since the day their high school football team won the regional championship. His teammates had hoisted him onto their shoulders so he could lift the trophy high to show the screaming crowd. The streaks in his hair had shone nearly as golden as the trophy, and she'd thought then that she'd never seen a young man look so fine.

He didn't take his eyes off the path of the plane,

but he reached over to touch the back of her hand, almost as though he were thanking her for letting him keep on flying.

The plane jolted up and down again and she swallowed hard, but there was no way she would make him turn back.

"Look down to your right," Robbie said. "Those two buildings on the top of that mountain are The Aerie and Adam Bosch's house. You can see the helipad in the clearing nearby."

Holly braced herself to look down. The top of the mountain was closer than she expected which she found comforting rather than terrifying. It took her a minute to figure out what she was looking at but then her perspective adjusted and she saw the structures Robbie was talking about. "They look so different from above," she said. "You can see the way the road connects everything and how it winds down the mountain to the highway. I never knew how it all fit together."

She turned back to Robbie to find him grinning. "Now you understand."

She understood up to a point. The scenery wasn't quite compelling enough to make her give up her death grip on the seatbelts.

"Let's see if you can find your own house," Robbie said, banking the airplane left.

A mew of distress escaped from her as the world tilted wildly again.

"Sorry." Robbie eased the plane into a gentler turn. "This baby is so maneuverable I forget not to fly like a stunt pilot."

As they approached the town of Sanctuary, Holly found herself glued to the window so she could puzzle out familiar landmarks from this unique perspective. "That's the Baptist church," she crowed, recognizing the distinctive red and tan shingles on the roof. "And the cemetery. I see Washington Street." That anchored the rest of the town and suddenly she could find anything she wanted to.

"There's my house!" She recognized it by the gazebo in the back yard since the roofs all looked almost identical in the housing development. She was struck by how small and close-together it all appeared.

Robbie pointed out the Boone farm on the other side of the highway and then traced along the Limestone River toward Flat Top Mountain. "Call Claire and tell her to bring the girls outside. We'll give them a wing wave."

"I thought you weren't supposed to use a phone in a plane," Holly said, as she pulled her cell phone out of her pocket.

"It's fine." Robbie winked. "If it messes up the navigation, I know where I am."

"I guess that's true," Holly said, admiring the shining ribbon of water winding through the valley.

Claire answered the phone. "I thought you were flying,"

"I am." Holly felt a burst of pride at how calmly she could say that. "We're about to fly over your house. Bring the girls outside."

As the big house Tim had built halfway up the mountain came into view, Robbie let the plane drift downward until she could see three figures standing on the back deck.

"I'm going to do a wing wobble now," Robbie warned.

Holly nodded, her attention on her family members below.

The plane rocked side-to-side several times, as Holly waved at Claire, Brianna, and Kayleigh. "Do you think they can see me?" she asked.

"No, but you can tell them you waved." He banked the plane away from the mountain. "I'll make another pass."

He brought the plane even lower this time, giving the girls the same wing signal. Holly thought she could see Kayleigh jump up and down. "Thank you for that," she said, as they gained altitude again. She hoped her daughters would think of her as adventurous. Not that she had told them she was afraid of flying; she didn't want to put fear of any kind in their minds.

"I'm going to show you my favorite view now," Robbie said. He steered the plane away from Flat Top Mountain and began to climb. The winter sun burned through a sky so blue its intensity made her blink. After several minutes of upward flight, the plane leveled off.

"Look down," Robbie said.

The river had shrunk to a mere golden thread, and the trees and snow covering the mountains looked like gray and white velvet draped over the underlying rock. She scanned forward to find ridge after ridge running horizontally beneath them as they sailed through the high blue sky. The world seemed both smaller and larger as it spread out under the plane.

"The only limit is the amount of gas in the tank," Robbie said, his eyes on the horizon. "And we've got a thousand miles before we run out of that."

Suddenly she understood. Up here, he felt freed of the constraints Sanctuary and his family had laid on him.

"It's beautiful," she said. "No boundaries."

He nodded before turning to her. "Want to take the control stick?" he asked with a look that invited her to share his joy.

No, she didn't want to touch that stick but she wasn't going to admit it. "If you're sure I won't crash the plane."

"We're up high enough so I can fix any mistake you make before we hit anything." He gave her a smile. "Put your hand on the stick and just feel how I'm moving it. Don't try to steer it yourself yet."

She took in a deep breath and gingerly wrapped her fingers around the joystick beside her seat. It vibrated and swayed as Robbie made small adjustments to keep the plane level and straight.

"Now see what happens when I move it this way." He pushed it gently sideways and the plane tilted slightly before he moved the stick back. "Now forward."

She began to anticipate what the plane's response would be as Robbie manipulated the control in various directions, steering the plane through several gentle turns and circles. Her hand relaxed into a more natural grip on the stick and she started to move with it.

"Take over," Robbie said, taking his hand off the control and dropping it onto his thigh.

"What!" Holly's fingers convulsed on the joystick and the plane's nose rose sharply.

"Ease it forward," Robbie said, his hand still on his thigh.

She shoved the stick away from her and the nose plunged.

"A little less forward." Robbie's voice was unruffled.

She adjusted the stick slowly back and the craft righted itself. She breathed in and out to dispel the panic adrenalin.

"Robbie McGraw, you scared the heck out of me," she scolded.

"You've been flying the plane for the past five minutes and didn't even know it," he said, his grin flashing. "I was just resting my hand on the stick to make you think I was steering."

"Seriously?"

He nodded and crossed his arms over his chest.

She kept the plane straight and level for a few minutes. Then she began to give it little nudges in one direction or another. "Can I turn it in a circle?"

"Go right ahead."

Carefully, she moved the stick until the left wing tilted up slightly and the plane began to bank. She held it steady, making tiny adjustments to keep it on a smooth path.

"Nice work," Robbie said as she brought it back level again. "Now turn it the other way."

She made a tighter circle this time.

"Now do a loop-the-loop," he said after she straightened out.

"Not funny." She flexed her fingers around the grip, noticing the slight dampness of perspiration on her palm. "And don't you do one either."

He chuckled. "Turn her south, and we'll head back to the airport."

"Which way's south?"

Robbie pointed to one of the screens on the dashboard and explained how to fly by the compass.

Soon she began to recognize landmarks and a sense of regret nipped at her. "I guess it's time for you to take over. I don't think I'm ready to land the plane yet."

Wrapping his fingers around the joystick, Robbie said, "Take a lesson or two and you will be. You're a natural born pilot."

Gratification rolled through her. "I don't know about that, but it's fun."

His eyes rivaled the brilliance of the sky when he turned to face her. "I knew you'd feel that way."

He clearly didn't know her very well because she was shocked at herself. She'd expected to grit her teeth and get through the ride with Robbie. The thought of actually flying the plane had been as remote as the prospect of walking on the moon. Yet she hadn't wanted to give up the controls.

"How about we have a little fun with the descent?" Robbie asked.

"What does that mean?"

"I'll take her down in a spiral."

The old Holly would have wanted a straight, gradual descent, but she grabbed her seatbelt with both hands and said, "Go for it."

CHAPTER NINE

"That was amazing! I didn't know a plane could even do that." Holly vibrated with excitement as she climbed into Robbie's Dodge Ram. "And I sure didn't think I could fly a plane."

"I'm pretty sure you could do anything you put your mind to," Robbie said before he closed the door he was holding for her.

She stored his comment away to think about later as she waited for him to come around and swing into the driver's seat. "How high can that plane go?" she asked.

"Twenty-five thousand feet." He backed out of the parking space.

"Have you ever been that high?"

"Once or twice." He took his eyes off the road to slant her a smile. "Crystal's already rubbing her hands together at the thought of all the flying lessons you're going to take."

She couldn't afford flying lessons, but that didn't

take away from how elated she was about her experience. "I didn't expect it to be so…so thrilling. Wait till I tell the girls I flew the plane. Even Claire will be impressed."

She felt so different. She, Holly Snedegar, elementary school secretary and divorced single mom, had flown an airplane the first time she'd ever been in one. It wasn't that she thought she was now a competent pilot. It was that she'd fought through her fear to try out something far outside her comfort zone… and she'd succeeded. What a gift Robbie had given her!

"Robbie, you are…"

She turned to look at him. His hands rested on the steering wheel with a sure but relaxed grip. The leather of his jacket pulled tight over the muscles of his arm as he steered around a curve in the highway.

The excitement thrumming through her body took on a whole new quality. It transformed itself into a desire to run her fingers over the muscles outlined by the jacket and an even deeper yearning to have his hands glide over her body the way they did the truck's steering wheel.

He glanced at her. "I am what?"

"You are…" She couldn't find the right words to describe everything he was, so she switched gears. "Do you ever go somewhere else and land?"

"I've gone up to Maryland to eat fresh crab and down to Georgia to pick up ripe peaches. Maybe you'd like to take a ride and have lunch somewhere. What's your favorite food?"

Nancy Herkness

"Italian. Can you fly me to Tuscany?"

He chuckled. "I'll see if I can borrow a 747." He turned onto Cornsilk Lane. "I hear there's a real good Italian restaurant in Greensboro. How about that as a substitute?"

"I'd love that." The prospect of another flight with him sent joyful anticipation bubbling through her. She wanted to bounce up and down in her seat like Kayleigh.

He pulled the truck into her driveway and killed the engine.

Now came the really nerve-racking part of the day. She tried to figure out how to choreograph her seduction. Did she lead him into the bedroom? Or snuggle up to him on the sofa?

Nerves tied her stomach into a knot. The thought of taking off her clothes in front of Robbie McGraw made all the confidence she thought she'd built up from flying the airplane evaporate like snow in June. Not even the sexy lingerie Claire had bought for her could bolster it back up again.

She opened the truck door and slid out before Robbie could get around to help her. Her high-heeled boots skidded on an ice patch as she started for the house.

"Careful there." Robbie reached her in time for her to stumble against the solid wall of his body. Her embarrassment vanished as yearning spiraled through her.

She looked up and found his eyes blazing with the same fire that licked along her nerve endings.

She waited for him to lower his head and meet her lips with his, but he took a step away and turned her toward the sidewalk. "Let's get you indoors before you take a tumble."

She hoped he hadn't noticed her expecting his kiss.

He walked beside her up the steps to her front door and stood aside as she unlocked it. Gesturing her through first, he closed the door behind them and shot the deadbolt home.

Unbuttoning her coat, she turned and said, "Would you like a—? Oh!"

He wrapped one arm around her waist and pulled her close as he slid his other hand into her hair to angle her head. "I'm sorry, Holly," he said. "I've wanted to do this all afternoon."

He bent his neck and his lips touched hers. It was a claiming kiss, hot and intense with all the pent-up desire he'd been holding in. Her bones seemed to melt, and she slid her hands under his jacket so she could press her palms against his back. She dug her fingers into the muscles of his shoulders to hold on as he tilted her head back to drag his mouth down her throat and lick the hollow at the base. The swirl of warmth and moisture made her gasp and pulse her hips against him.

"Yes," he rasped, sliding one of his hands down to cup her bottom and pull her in so she could feel his erection.

He held her there while he kissed her eyebrows, her eyelids, her cheeks, her mouth, and her neck.

The contrast between his light sensual kisses and the pressure of his hand holding her against his hard arousal sent heat searing through her to coil deep in her belly.

She wanted—no, she *needed*—more contact. She wound her arms around his neck and said, "Lift me!" as she gave a little jump. His hands went to her waist and she wrapped her legs around his hips, her skirt hiking up so her lace panties met the denim of his jeans in a near-explosion of sensation. They both moaned at the same time.

He turned so that her back came up against the wall of the little foyer. Then he shifted his hands to her thighs. "Holly!" he breathed as his palms found the bare skin above her thigh-high stockings. His fingers curled around to caress the soft inner skin.

She arched into the wall to rub herself harder against his erection, as the tension inside her wound tighter. He helped her by grinding his hips between her spread legs as he devoured her mouth.

It wasn't enough. She wedged her hands down between them to rip the buttons of his shirt open, spreading her fingers over the skin of his chest. She wanted to feel that warm wall of muscle against her breasts, so she began to pull at her blouse.

"No," Robbie said, shocking her into looking back up. A wicked smile curved his lips. "I want to undress you."

He reached back to unhook her legs from his waist so she slid down his body. Her feet had barely touched the floor before he wrapped his arm around her waist and hustled her through the living room and down the hall to her bedroom. She refused to think about the reason he knew every room in her house. She didn't want her ugly past to sully this moment.

Once in her bedroom, he kept moving until they were beside the bed. Bracing one of his knees on the mattress, he lowered her backwards until she was lying down, looking up into his fiercely blue eyes.

"Don't move," he said, straightening to shrug out of his jacket and his shirt so his torso was bare.

This was perfect. He would undress for her, and she could keep her clothes on.

"You're so beautiful," she breathed, lifting her hands to trace the sharply defined muscles of his abdomen before she skimmed over the golden brown hair tracing a line down to the waistband of his jeans. His muscles contracted but he let her continue to explore until she thumbed his nipples.

Then he pushed her back on the bed as his fingers went to the buttons of her blouse. She still wore her winter coat and he had to move it aside as he flicked open the first button. Blessing Claire for the pushup bra, she watched his face while he worked his way downward. His gaze went sharp as the cream silk slid away from the red lace.

Pulling the hem from her skirt to reach the last button, he took the edges of silk and spread them apart, pushing the coat open farther at the same time. Her breath quickened as her lace-covered breasts were exposed to him.

"This is what I wanted." He stared down at her.

It was what she wanted too, except his intent gaze was beginning to remind her of the shortcomings of her body. She shifted nervously. He was still holding her blouse so the backs of his fingers brushed against the sides of her breasts.

Her eyelids slammed shut to savor the flare of sensation.

Then his fingers were on her shoulders, shoving the coat and blouse down before he dragged them off her arms and tossed them on the floor. He braced his palms on either side of her and bent to bring his mouth to the swell of her breasts, tracing his tongue along the edge of the filmy red lace.

She let him tease her for a moment or two before taking his head between her hands and guiding his lips to her hard, aching nipples. She threaded her fingers into his hair and held on as he sucked on her, making the lace hot and damp against her skin. A rope of desire burned straight from her breasts to spin in an ever-tightening knot of arousal between her thighs.

She shuddered and arched against him, making his teeth graze the exquisitely sensitive peak. An orgasm hovered but she fought it back.

He slipped his hands behind her and unhooked her bra, pulling it down her arms and tossing it away. Then his palms were cupping her bare breasts as he stared down at her, his jaw tight with control.

The feel of his skin against hers nearly sent her over the edge again, so she ripped his belt buckle open and went to work on the snap of his jeans.

He huffed out a raspy laugh. "I'm trying to take it slow."

"Maybe next time." She yanked his zipper down so his erection pushed out under the black briefs he wore.

He helped her out by toeing off his boots and shoving down his briefs and jeans. She lay back and took in the sight of the sculpted lines down the front of his thighs and the flex of his buttocks as he bent to rip off his socks.

He put one knee on the bed again, and reached for the buckle of her slim belt. As she watched the fluid slide of his muscles under his skin, she thought of her own body.

Her stomach rounded outward no matter how many crunches she did. There was a scar from the Caesarean she'd had for Kayleigh. Her sun-starved skin was so pale it was nearly blue.

Robbie was so perfect. He wouldn't want her.

She reached for his hands to stop him, but he misinterpreted her gesture, thinking she wanted to hurry him. He caught her wrists and stretched them above her head, bending so his chest brushed her nipples, making pleasure flare so she involuntarily arched up against him.

"I want to unwrap you," he said, his eyes locked on hers. "Like a Christmas gift."

All she could manage was a tiny whimper of agreement. As long as he was hiding her body with his, she was happy to have nothing covering her so she could feel his touch. He released her wrists and ran his hands down the length of her arms until she felt his fingers at her belt buckle.

She closed her eyes as her belt was whipped out of its loops with a whisper of leather against fabric. He found the button on the side of her skirt and slid the zipper down. She lifted her hips so he could pull her skirt down. As the fabric slithered past her knees, he made a strangled sound that startled her into opening her eyes.

He stood with her skirt dangling from one hand, his eyes blazing with desire. He dropped the skirt and bent to trace the tops of her thigh-high stockings with both hands. "I'm leaving these and the boots on," he rasped, his gaze following the path of his fingertips.

A wave of feminine power surged through her as she saw his erection tighten. His exploration drifted around to her inner thighs and she moaned, spreading her legs to give him access to the place that ached for his touch.

Then he knelt, and she could no longer see his face. She was about to tilt her head up when she felt his fingers at the sides of her panties, moving them down carefully over the stockings and then swiftly down the boots. She closed her eyes and grabbed fistfuls of quilt to keep from covering herself with her hands.

Her hold on the quilt convulsed when she felt his lips press against the inside of her thigh and his fingers slide between her legs and inside her. He murmured something against her, the whiff of his breath stroking her skin, and then she lost all thought as his thumb touched the center of her ache. She lifted her hips to offer him more of herself and he accepted, moving his mouth to where his thumb had been. She whimpered in protest as his fingers came out of her, but then he flexed them around her behind, holding her so he could use his mouth and tongue to wind her closer and closer to orgasm.

Now her desire was wound so tightly that she no longer cared what he thought of her. She simply wanted him to release her into an orgasm.

"Robbie," she begged, releasing the quilt to thread her fingers in his hair. All sensation focused on his touch between her legs, but she ached to have him inside her before she exploded over the edge. "Robbie!" With a supreme effort, she curled her torso upward to see his blue eyes glazed with arousal. "Come with me."

"I wanted to give you this first," he said, lifting his head.

She shook her head. "Together."

He let her hips down on the bed and bent to grab his jeans, pulling a condom out of the pocket and ripping the packet open with his teeth.

"Let me." Holly held out her hand. "I want to touch you."

He stood and took her hand to pull her to a sitting position before handing her the condom. She couldn't resist running a finger along a ridge of muscle in his abdomen, pulling a low groan from him before she rolled the condom onto his erection. The moment she was done, he tumbled her back onto the bed, moving her into the center as he stretched out over her and settled between her legs.

He twined his fingers with hers and braced himself on his elbows, bending to kiss her at the same time as he flexed his hips to thrust inside her. The combination of his lips against hers, his chest brushing her sensitized breasts, and his cock filling and stretching her sent her into a bursting climax. She cried out against his mouth, bowing up off the bed as the waves of release slammed over her.

He went still, allowing the aftershocks to ripple through her before he began to move again, slowly and steadily, fanning the heat inside her into a spark and then a flame. His mouth was against the side of her neck, his tongue tracing a path of delicious warmth over her skin. He nipped at her, the sharp edge of his teeth sending a frisson of excitement dancing over her skin and into her belly. She tightened her internal muscles around him, making him growl and pick up his rhythm.

She wrapped her legs around his waist, angling her hips so he could seat himself more deeply each time. He thrust fast and hard before he arched up, straightening his arms and throwing his head back as he ground out her name in a hoarse shout.

As he pumped inside her, he rotated his hips and sent her blasting into another orgasm.

And then he was rolling over with her body cradled against his, so she ended up sprawled on top of him, his chest rising and falling under her cheek while his breath whistled past her ear.

She lay there, letting her senses take in all the textures and angles of his body where it touched hers. The crush of her breasts against the heat and solidity of his chest. The weight of his arms loosely crossed over her back, his fingertips tickling her ribs just slightly. The rough hair and hard muscle of his thigh where her legs brushed on either side. Without lifting her head, she slid her fingers up to trace the strong bone of his jaw, feeling the contrast of skin and the smallest hint of stubble.

She felt him twist his head and then his lips were on her fingers, adding a moist heat to the swirl of feeling. The satisfied glow inside her flickered and then subsided again. Two orgasms in a row had wrung her out.

Robbie's breathing settled into a normal rhythm, and he rolled again, letting her slide off him and onto the bed. She sighed in complaint at the loss of contact.

"I'll be right back." He yanked a couple of tissues out of the box on the bedside table and disposed of the condom.

She expected him to come back to the bed, but he stood looking down at her before he huffed out a sigh and bent to unzip one of the boots she'd forgotten she still wore. "I hate to take these off," he said, slipping it from her foot, "but you'll be more comfortable without them."

She remembered wrapping her legs around his

hips quite tightly and a flush climbed her cheeks. "I hope I didn't dig the heels into you."

He grinned as he unzipped the second boot and pulled it off. "Not that I noticed."

"Turn around."

"It's fine," he said, pulling the quilt out from under her before he slid under it beside her. He wrapped an arm around her waist and pulled her back in close against him, bringing his lips to the tender skin just below her ear lobe. "You smell so good." He inhaled and blew out a warm breath before he kissed her. "You feel so good." His tongue flicked out. "You taste so good."

Holly shivered at the progression of sensation. "You *are* good," she said.

His arm tightened around her. "With you I am."

Her eyelids fluttered closed as she luxuriated in the knowledge that her body pleased Robbie. It might be just the novelty, but for now, she was exciting to him, and it made her feel powerful in a purely feminine way.

Now that they'd gotten past the first shock of intimacy, she wanted to spend the rest of their evening and night together exploring his body, seeing how they fit together, finding the places he enjoyed being touched. And she was sure he would find the same places on her.

She reached down and took the hand he had splayed over her hip, moving it up to cup her breast. She felt his cock jump against her backside as the breath hissed through his teeth.

"Are you sure?" he rasped.

She answered by circling her hips against him.

He didn't ask any more questions for a long time.

CHAPTER TEN

Robbie tried to focus on the bite of mince pie he'd just put in his mouth, but all his attention centered on Holly sitting across the candlelit table from him. The flickering light reflected in her dark eyes and ran along strands of her waving hair like liquid fire. He'd never seen a woman look so sexy in just a white blouse. Of course, it helped that she wasn't wearing a bra under the thin silk. He'd taken full advantage of that as she stood at the sink in the kitchen, fitting his body against her back and snaking his hands around to cup her full breasts and tease her nipples to points.

The memory made his cock get hard all over again.

She was watching him with a question in her eyes, so he forced himself to chew, setting loose the flavor of fruit, nuts, and spices combined with melt-in-your-mouth buttery crust. "Grady's going to love this, and Adam Bosch is going to want a hundred," he said. "My mother couldn't have made it better."

She looked relieved. "I fiddled with the recipe so I wasn't sure if it worked."

"Oh, it works." He took another forkful as she lifted her wineglass to her lips. Her every movement reminded him of touching her somewhere on that gorgeous body. He'd been fantasizing about her for months in ways that made him feel guilty. But after she'd invited him to join her in the shower this afternoon, his fantasies paled next to the reality.

The guilt had only gotten worse though.

Before he'd been able to tell himself he admired her as a beautiful, courageous mother of two children. His fantasies were not reality. Now he knew what her skin felt like under his hands, how she moaned in the back of her throat when he touched her, the way her eyes widened and then closed as she neared her climax. She had given herself to him with a generosity that took his breath away. He had taken everything she offered, knowing he had nothing permanent to give her in return.

But that wasn't the real problem.

He ached to spend the night making love to her until they both collapsed in exhaustion, and then wake up with her naked in his arms so he could make love to her again. And he wanted to do it every night for the rest of their lives. But he was leaving and her life was firmly rooted in Sanctuary.

He needed to end this before either one of them got in any deeper.

He devoured the rest of the pie and stood up

with his plate in his hand. "I'll help you wash up and then I'd better go."

She looked as though he'd just thrown ice water in her face. "You don't have to leave yet. The girls are spending the night at Claire's."

He knew that. "I don't want folks seeing my truck parked in your driveway and drawing conclusions that might hurt you."

Her face cleared and a mischievous glint shone in her eyes. "We can put it in the garage. Or better yet, park it four doors down in front of that old busybody Bertha Shanks' house. She'll go crazy wondering who you're staking out."

He realized he owed Holly the truth, so he sat back down. "There's something I need to tell you."

It looked as though someone had closed the shutters over the face of the sparkling woman he'd been watching. She was bracing herself for the emotional hit. He imagined she'd learned this from her time with her ex-husband, and it made his guilt expand exponentially.

He tried to figure out how to sugarcoat his news but he decided the bald truth was the best way to handle it. "I've accepted a job with the police department in Atlanta, and I'll be leaving Sanctuary at the end of January."

He was baffled when both relief and guilt showed on her face. She nodded. "I know. I overheard you talking with Paul in Grady's barn the other evening."

That rocked him back in his chair. He struggled

to rearrange his thoughts around this information.

Holly looked down at her hands, folded on the table. "Maybe it makes me a bad person, but I wanted this to happen, even though I knew you were leaving." She lifted her gaze back to his. "I feel like a woman again. Not a failure."

The honesty of her socked him in the gut. "Frank was the failure, not you."

Now she turned to stare at the Christmas tree although he was sure she wasn't seeing the reflection of the lights on the tinsel. "When someone you love tells you over and over again that you're no good, you start to believe it. And then you feel like a weak-minded fool when you finally realize it's not true. But the belief has taken root somewhere so deep inside you that you can't quite dig it out."

"Holly—" He reached across the table to lay his hand on top of hers.

She turned her palm up to wrap her fingers around his as she summoned a smile. "It's okay. I'm okay. I just needed this one last piece to put myself back together again. Thank you."

She was thanking him for some of the greatest sex he'd ever had? He had to fix this. "You've got it backwards. I don't deserve to touch the hem of your skirt, but I've gotten to taste your lips and kiss your breasts and come inside you. I'm the one who's grateful."

Her face took on a glow. She leaned across the table toward him and whispered in a husky voice, "Robbie, I want you inside me right now."

His cock turned to iron and he shifted in his chair as he shook his head. "It's not right for me to do this. You're not the kind of woman you have a one-night stand with."

"Let me pretend for tonight. I want to be that kind of woman just once in my life."

Robbie caught the uncertainty that still lived in her eyes. He wanted to punch Frank out, but even more, he wanted to uproot the doubt and insecurity the bastard had inflicted on this incredible woman.

For tonight, Robbie would be the kind of man who took advantage of Holly's offer.

He shoved back his chair and came around the table to lift Holly out of hers. Carrying her to the sofa, he looked down to see her cloud of dark hair spilling over his arm, her eyes half-closed with anticipation while a wicked smile curved her lips.

He turned his gaze toward the ceiling. "Imagine there's a whole hedge of mistletoe hanging over this couch because I'm going to kiss every inch of your body under it."

CHAPTER ELEVEN

Holly flipped the pancakes over in the cast iron skillet, the fragrance of hot sweet batter wafting around her. One flapjack landed on the countertop because her mind was distracted by images of the man currently using her shower. She scraped the errant disk up and tossed it into the sink, pouring a fresh circle of batter on the griddle.

She stood watching the pancakes bubble as she remembered how it felt to run her hands over Robbie's water-slicked skin. She'd overcome his scruples and persuaded him to stay the night, so they woke up tangled in each other's arms this morning. Then they'd gotten even more tangled before he had to get ready to fly Santa to the hospital. Her body hummed with bone-deep satisfaction and feminine energy.

She really was turning into a bad person, because she didn't feel guilty about any of it.

The sound of running water ceased. She loaded

the pancakes onto one of her precious Christmas china plates and slid it in the warm oven. The bacon was cooked to the perfect crispiness, and a homemade coffee cake, dusted with powdered sugar, stood on the table. She poured the warm maple syrup into a small glazed pitcher made by a local potter and set it on the red-and-green plaid tablecloth.

She heard footsteps and then Robbie appeared in the kitchen doorway in the same clothes he'd worn the day before, his damp hair still showing comb marks. She felt her lips curve into a smile of welcome. "Hope you're hungry."

He didn't answer her smile with one of his own, and her spirits plummeted. She turned to pull the pancakes out of the oven, adding bacon before she carried it to the table.

"Holly, I feel like crap about this."

"Don't," she said. "Just eat."

He shook his head. "What I did isn't right."

A spurt of anger straightened her spine and she whirled to face him. "Every single thing you did was right, so right I can't stop thinking about it. Don't you make it sound bad!"

He raked his fingers through his hair, destroying the neat lines the comb had left. "You were so beautiful up there in that plane, and so alive."

Holly nodded, wanting him to know she'd felt the same way. "It was like electricity between us. Like we could have powered the plane just on that." The blue of his eyes glowed and she knew he was remembering the energy crackling around the cockpit. "It had to go somewhere, Robbie, so it went into making love."

"I knew I was leaving in a few weeks, and I thought you didn't."

The man was too honorable for his own good. She heard the exasperation in her voice as she said, "I knew exactly what I was doing. I don't wear red lace lingerie on a daily basis."

A pained smile twisted his lips. "Yeah, but I've pictured you in it every day."

Gratification rolled through her, quelling the irritation. "That's what I like to hear."

He shook his head. "You're not that kind of woman."

"Why can't I be? Just for one month with you."

He thrust his hands into the pockets of his jeans. "Because you're the kind of woman you tell your troubles to every night when you come home. The kind you have babies with and waltz around the dance floor at your fiftieth wedding anniversary party."

She wanted to clap her hand over his mouth and tell him to stop but he kept on talking.

"You're a once-in-a-lifetime kind of woman. I may kick myself for throwing this away, but I need to get beyond that nearest ridge of mountains." He looked down. "I'm afraid I won't go if I spend a month with you."

Comprehension rocked her back on her heels. He saw her as another woman like his mother and his sisters, winding herself around him to hold him back from the life in the outside world that he craved. "I promise to push you out the door when the time comes for your new job. I have my sister and Tim, my friends, a whole community who support me. I'll be fine."

"It wouldn't be you who would hold me back." He raised his gaze to hers. "I can't afford to get in any deeper."

She saw regret and doubt and longing in his eyes. She could play on those emotions to get him to stay with her and her daughters. He might even be happy, and he wouldn't leave her because he was decent down to the marrow of his bones. But he would always wonder what it would have been like to fly away from Sanctuary, always have that yearning that couldn't be satisfied. And she would never do that to this man she loved.

The realization sucked all the air out of her lungs and she gasped. Robbie was no longer a light flirtation or a means to make herself feel like an attractive woman again. She loved him with every ounce of her being. It had begun a year or so ago over those evening slices of pie in her kitchen and now their night together had fanned the warm flicker of affection into a full-blown conflagration that threatened to consume her heart.

She swallowed the clot of tears rising in her throat. She had to make him believe his words hadn't just about destroyed her. He had done so much for her; she owed him his freedom and a clear conscience. She nodded. "You're right. No reason to make it hard on either one of us." She forced a cheery tone into her voice. "I know you have to go, but there's no reason to leave hungry. Sit down and have some hotcakes while they're still hot."

"I'd better take a rain check on that." He crossed the space between them and framed her face with his hands. "I'll never forget being with you. Every single second is burned into my memory." He bent and pressed a gentle kiss to her lips and then released her. Before she could find her voice again, he had pivoted on his heel and walked out the kitchen door.

"Good-bye," she whispered. Then she sank down into a chair, folding her arms on the table so she could pillow her head as sobs wracked her body.

CHAPTER TWELVE

"*Dashing through the snow...*" Holly forced herself to sing along with Brianna and Kayleigh as they drove up the gravel road to Grady's farm. Not that she felt festive at the moment. She kept seeing Robbie's broad back disappearing through her kitchen door over and over again.

Kayleigh stopped singing. "Mama, look how pretty the nativity scene is with the snow on top of it!"

There'd been a snowstorm during the night, as Robbie had predicted, and she'd been worried her mini-van wouldn't make it up the drive. But Grady had plowed it down to just an inch of powder. Holly cast a quick sideways glance at the decorations. Most of the figures were buried knee deep in the white stuff, although it looked like a couple had been dug out. Maybe she would come down to finish the job it appeared Grady had started. Some hard physical labor might distract her from the tears that kept threatening to spill over.

"*Oh-oh! Jingle bells, jingle bells, jingle all the way.*" She joined the girls for the chorus, finishing just as they pulled up beside Grady's door. "Brianna, will you grab the pie carrier? Kayleigh, you can bring the cookie tin."

Claire had brought the girls home at lunchtime and sensed something was wrong with Holly, whispering, "Tell me when you're ready to talk about it," before she announced she was staying to help bake Christmas cookies. Holly wasn't ready yet, but she gave her sister a grateful hug and a watery smile.

Claire's supportive presence and her daughters' excitement about the upcoming holiday lifted Holly's mood. As the delicious holiday aroma of hot sugar and butter swirled through the kitchen, Holly told her sister and her children about her first experience in the sky. When she saw the respect and wonder shining in her daughters' eyes as she told them she'd been in control of the plane for part of the flight, she felt a rush of pride that put a temporary bandage over the pain of losing Robbie.

Now they had come back to earth to deliver fresh cookies and the promised mince pie to the elderly farmer. Holly hoped to make it a quick trip so she could go home and take a nap and probably cry some more in the privacy of her bedroom. She and Robbie hadn't slept much the night before. She hoped fatigue didn't sabotage his ability to fly Santa's helicopter.

They knocked on the door and waited, but there was no answer and no sound or movement came from within the house.

"Let's try the barn," Holly said.

"I hope Noël's inside so we can visit her." Brianna gave a little skip.

Holly was worried Noël might hurt one of them after the incident where the donkey had knocked her into Robbie. Not that she minded the contact with him, but Noël seemed so capricious. She was worried about Brianna or Kayleigh getting stepped on or bowled over. And she couldn't forget those big square teeth. "We'll just pat her from outside the stall though."

Brianna looked disappointed.

"Grady?" Holly called as they opened the barn door and slipped inside.

"Mr. Boone?" Kayleigh's high little voice echoed in the rafters.

An ear-splitting hee-haw shattered the stillness of the barn. Holly jumped and grabbed Brianna's shoulder as her heart did a flip in her chest.

"That's just Noël saying hello, Mama."

"I know. She has a loud voice though." Holly took the pie and cookies from the girls and set them on a hay bale before they walked down to the donkey's stall. Noël's head was already over the half-door, her ears pointed toward them. She lifted her head and let out another thunderous bray. Holly was braced for it this time, but the sound still made her wince as it walloped into her eardrums.

Brianna and Kayleigh, on the other hand, broke into a run to reach the donkey faster. As Holly caught up with them, they were already cooing over

Noël, stroking her nose and neck and scratching behind her long, graceful ears. Holly had to admit the donkey was a pretty little thing, but she sure had an ugly voice.

"Look, Mama, she's wearing a jacket." Kayleigh pointed to the red and green horse blanket buckled around Noël's neck and belly.

Holly took a quick glance. "She looks very stylish. You two stay right here. I'm going to look for Mr. Boone." She gave them a listen-to-your-mother look. "No going in the stall."

"Yes, ma'am," the girls agreed obediently, but without enthusiasm.

Holly searched the barn, checking the workshop, the loft, and the feed room, but Grady was nowhere to be found. She and the girls went outside to walk around the house and barn, calling his name. His truck was parked in the garage and the tractor was in the barn, so he had to be somewhere within walking distance.

Holly stood in the middle of the road, her hands on her hips, as she debated where to look. She hated to invade the privacy of his house but a niggle of worry snagged in her throat. He was an elderly man and he'd shoveled a lot of snow that morning. "Let's see if the side door's unlocked," she said, making her decision.

The knob turned in her hand. Easing it open, she stuck her head inside and called Grady's name into the empty mudroom. Her voice was swallowed by the silence of an empty house.

"I don't think he's home, Mama," Kayleigh said.

"Probably not, but I want to make sure." Holly pushed the door wide and herded the girls inside. "Wipe your boots really well."

Peering into the kitchen, she heaved a sigh of relief when she didn't find Grady's body crumpled on the floor. "You two have a seat at the table while I see if Grady's upstairs and can't hear us." If the farmer had collapsed, she didn't want the girls to discover him.

The girls seemed to sense her concern because they sat at the Formica-topped metal table without argument.

Holly walked swiftly through the old farmhouse, finding the square rooms a mish-mash of several decades of decorating trends. Yet the hand-quilted throw pillows somehow perfectly accented the blunt-edged sofa upholstered in a 60s-vintage stripe. Bess had had an artistic eye.

Finding no sign of Grady downstairs, she put her foot on the bottom step of the staircase and took a deep breath before she called upward. "Grady? Are you here?"

When there was no answer, she jogged up the stairs and made a swift tour of the second floor. No sign of Grady.

"Where could he be?" Brianna asked when Holly returned to the kitchen. Her voice held some of the worry Holly felt.

The only place she could think of was the nativity scene. She remembered noticing he hadn't finished clearing the figures. *What if he hadn't been able to?*

"Let's get in the van," she said, the urgency in her voice sending her daughters scrambling off their chairs and out the door.

They got buckled into their seats in record time and she pointed the mini-van back down the road. "If you see any footprints leading off the road, you shout out." She was scanning back and forth along the sides of the drive herself. The fresh snow would show those clearly, and her girls had eagle eyes.

As they came alongside the gate leading to the field where the nativity scene stood, Brianna said, "I see footprints leading into the field."

Holly had spotted them too. She slammed the van into park and turned off the engine. "You two stay here and keep warm."

"But—" Kayleigh started to protest, but Brianna shushed her.

"Mama needs to go fast, and we can't keep up in the snow."

Holly jumped out of the van and ran to the gate. Unlatching it, she pushed it open along the track Grady must have made, a short arc of scraped snow ending in a pile he'd used the gate to sweep aside. She left it unlatched and followed Grady's trail, stretching out her stride to set her boots into the fresh footprints. That way she could move through the deep snow more swiftly. Every now and then she lifted her gaze to scan ahead of her, hoping to see the farmer. She thought she remembered that the figures farther away from the gate were the ones he'd already shoveled out.

The trek across the snowy field seemed so much longer without Robbie striding along beside her. Her chest heaved as the frigid air set her lungs burning. She reached the first of the three wise men. "Grady? Are you here?" she called, stopping to look around more thoroughly.

"Holly! Here!" The farmer's hoarse cry came from near the grouping of shepherds at the far side of the nativity stable.

Holly forgot about the cold and her burning lungs as she high-stepped through the snow drifts. She passed the camels, the holy family, and the first sheep when she spotted Grady, propped up against a shepherd, his legs stretched out in front of him. "What happened? Where are you hurt?"

The old farmer untucked his gloved hands from under his armpits and gestured toward his left leg. She noticed his cheeks were so pale they were nearly white. "Wash…was…shoveling snow away from thish…this…shepherd when I b-blacked out or s-something. Ankle shtuck…stuck…under the shovel when I f-fell. W-won't hold me." A series of shivers racked his body and she could hear his teeth clatter together.

She was afraid the slurring she heard in his voice was from whatever had caused him to lose consciousness.

"How long have you been here?" Holly asked, shrugging her quilted coat off and draping it over

A Down-Home Country Christmas

Grady's chest and shoulders like a blanket. She unwound her scarf and wrapped it around his neck and chin. She knew he was truly cold when he didn't object.

"N-not sure." He shivered again. "Sh-should've brought my shell...cell...ph-phone. G-got out of the h-habit after B-Besh...Bess p-passed."

She needed to get him out of the snow and cold immediately. Holly surveyed Grady's height and breadth and realized she wouldn't be able to get him to the mini-van by herself. Nor would the van make it across the field in the snow. She thought of Grady's tractor, but even if she could figure out how to drive it, she couldn't lift him up onto it. The tractor reminded her of the barn and its most familiar inhabitant.

"Could Noël walk through this snow?" she asked the farmer.

Grady looked confused. "Y-you mean, the d-donkey? I g-guess sho...so. W-why?"

"Because you need a ride. I'll be back."

She reached into her jeans pocket for her cell phone and remembered she'd left it in the mini-van. Cursing under her breath, she started back toward the van, practically leapfrogging from one footprint to the next. Despite her exertions, the cold air was penetrating her thin sweater, turning the sweat she'd worked up into icy fingers on her skin. And she couldn't get enough of the thin air into her lungs. She remembered Grady's face and forced her burning thighs to lift higher and faster.

As she approached the gate, she saw the door of the mini-van slide open, and Brianna hopped out. "Mama, did you find him?"

"Yes," Holly managed to call out. "Get...blanket." Brianna disappeared back into the van.

Holly shoved the gate open, and Brianna emerged with the stadium blanket they kept stowed in back for football games and picnics. "Honey," Holly paused to suck in a breath of frigid air, "I'm going to ask you to do a grown-up job. Follow my footsteps over to the nativity scene and find Mr. Boone. He's sitting behind the shepherd with the green and yellow robe. Wrap the blanket around him and snuggle up under it, right up against him, to help keep him warm." Holly gulped in another breath.

"Yes, ma'am." Brianna nodded as she clutched the folded blanket to her chest.

"I'm going to get Noël so Mr. Boone can ride her out of the field." Holly pulled Brianna in for a quick hug and then turned her toward the gate. "I'll be right back."

As Brianna set out across the field, Holly leapt into the minivan, slamming the door and yanking her cell phone out of its dashboard clip. As she dialed 9-1-1, Kayleigh's small, tentative voice came from behind her. "Is everything okay, Mama?"

Holly twisted around in the seat to give her daughter's knee a quick squeeze. "It will be, sweetie." The dispatcher answered her call and she shifted forward again. "Hello, it's Holly Snedegar.

I'm at Grady Boone's farm on Route 60. He's fallen in the snow by the nativity scene and hurt his ankle so he can't walk out. He lost consciousness before but he's awake now and slurring his words. Send an ambulance."

"You got it, Mrs. Snedegar," the dispatcher said. "Stay on the line in case I need to ask you any more questions."

Holly slotted the phone into the clip and turned on the ignition, blasting the heat onto her chilled skin.

She debated driving down to the bottom of the farm road to turn around but decided it would be quicker to just back all the way to the barn.

"What's wrong with Mr. Boone?" Kayleigh asked in a quavering voice.

"He hurt his ankle, sweetie." Holly swiveled to guide the car carefully along the road. The last thing she wanted to do was end up stuck in a snowdrift. "He'll be okay, but we need to get him out of the field."

She concentrated on navigating a curve in the road before she said, "I'm getting Noël. I need you to go in Mr. Boone's house and stay there. You can watch the TV in his living room, if you want to. Can you do that for me?"

Kayleigh's eyes were wide and slightly teary, but she nodded.

"You're a good, brave girl. I'm proud of you."

Kayleigh nodded again. "I want Mr. Boone to be all right."

"We're going to make sure he is." Holly pressed hard on the gas as the road straightened out, making gravel ping against the underside of the van. She slammed on the brakes as they got to the side door of the house. She flung the car door open and helped Kayleigh out of the van and up the steps. Opening the side door, she gave her daughter a hug and a gentle nudge into the house. "Don't worry. I'll be back to get you."

She made sure the door was firmly latched before she bolted toward the barn. As she shoved the big door partly open, she nearly halted as she realized she was going to have to handle the donkey all by herself. What if the stubborn creature refused to leave her stall? Or bit Holly? Or kicked her so hard she couldn't walk?

"I have flown an airplane. I can lead a donkey," Holly muttered as she hustled toward Noël's stall. She grabbed the lead line hanging by the door and slipped inside.

Noël was placidly munching on the hay she'd pulled from the net. As Holly closed the door, the donkey swung her head around, a long stem of dried grass dangling from her lips. Holly made a wide circle around Noël's hindquarters. As she sidled up to her, she decided to let the donkey know what she wanted. "Noël, your master's in trouble and I really need you to cooperate. Can you do that for me?"

Holly stopped and stretched out to grab at the donkey's halter just as Noël turned back to the hay net. "Darn it," Holly said, forced to take a couple of more steps forward in the thick straw bedding to keep her balance. She leaned forward again. Noël pulled a mouthful of hay out of the net and turned her head hard into Holly's hand, making them both jump. "Ow! Sorry, girl. Didn't mean to smack you." After shaking her sore hand, she made herself tiptoe even closer and slipped her fingers under the halter's cheek strap. "Gotcha!"

Clipping the lead line onto the middle ring under Noël's chin, Holly copied the way she'd seen Brianna lead her. She stood way too close for comfort to those big, grinding teeth with her right hand gripping the rope under the donkey's chin and the rest of the line coiled in her left hand. "Okay, let's go. Giddy-up!"

The donkey looked at her and continued chewing the hay.

"If that's the way you're going to be." Holly clenched her fist around the rope and gave it a sharp tug. To her amazement, Noël took a step toward the door. "Yes!"

She pulled on the line again and started walking. "C'mon, girl."

The donkey came along beside her. "Oh, thank goodness."

She led Noël out of the stall and toward the barn door. After a few more uneventful steps, she felt all her fear and tension swirl away like dishwater down the drain. But now her worry about Grady crashed back over her.

She debated trying to get on the donkey's back

and ride her to the field, but decided she was more likely to fall off than speed up the journey. As she and Noël burst out into the brightness of sunlight reflecting off snow, she blinked a few times and then coaxed the donkey into a trot, jogging along beside her as they hit the cleared road.

At least running was warming her up again. Noël's hooves crunched rhythmically on the snowy gravel and her hay-scented breath made white clouds in the freezing air. As Holly settled into a steady speed, she was surprised at how comforting it was to have the donkey trotting alongside her. They made quick work of getting to the gate, but had to slow down when they hit the snowy field.

"Brianna! Grady! I'm coming!" Holly called out, wading through the snow and letting the donkey follow in the trail that was becoming more and more beaten down.

"Mr. Boone's sleeping," Brianna called back.

Holly knew that was a bad sign, so she picked up her pace, yanking at Noël's lead line. Amazingly, the donkey matched her speed.

When they arrived at the shepherd, Brianna was shaking the farmer whose head was canted back against the wooden figure. "Wake up, Mr. Boone."

For a terrible moment, Holly was afraid he had died, but his eyelids fluttered open. "B-Besh?"

"Grady! I brought Noël." Holly kept it simple. "You have to get on her."

"G-get on Noël?" He looked around in bewilderment.

Holly handed the lead line to Brianna. "Sweetie, you take the lead line and hold Noël still." She picked up the shovel lying beside Grady, jabbing it down into the snow. "Use this like a cane on this side and I'll be on your other side to help you get up."

He still looked confused, so she took his hand and wrapped it around the handle of the shovel. "Pull yourself up on this," she said, squatting beside him to wrap his other arm over her shoulder. "Bend your right leg in so you can stand up."

He nodded and shifted to bring his foot inward. As she scooted in closer, she felt him shudder with the cold. "Okay, up!"

She had no idea where the burst of strength came from but as she felt his weight pressing on her shoulders, she exploded upward, dragging him with her.

"Bring Noël up as close as you can," she told Brianna. Her mother's heart glowed with pride as her daughter calmly guided the donkey so close that Grady didn't have to take even a half-step to reach her. "Great job, sweetie! Now hold her still."

Holly considered the logistics a moment. "Grady, can you lie across her back diagonally and let me swing your right leg over her rear?"

"Th-think sho." He levered himself forward using her shoulder and the shovel. She shifted his leg to the other side of the donkey and then helped him scoot forward onto the center of Noël's back. He ground out a low groan as his injured foot banged into the donkey's leg. But the little creature never flinched. Only her ears moved, flicking back and forth to follow the voices as Brianna stroked her nose and murmured soothing words.

Grady grabbed the edges of the horse blanket and tried to brace himself upright, but he began to slide off to one side. As panic pounded at her, Holly seized his thigh. He kept tipping sideways. She braced her feet and threw her weight backwards so hard she was sure she would land flat on the snow. His slow-motion fall stopped.

"Grady, lie down on Noël's neck and wrap your arms around her," she said, leaning farther back to bring him upright. "I'll hold you."

Grady lay down and Holly got up against Noël's side, taking fistfuls of the farmer's jacket and holding onto him like a limpet. "Brianna, start walking Noël back to the gate."

"Yes, ma'am," the girl said, as she set the donkey moving.

Holly staggered as she tried to slog through the deep snow alongside the trail. The gate looked miles away.

Brianna muttered under her breath.

Holly was instantly concerned. She was asking a lot of her eleven-year-old daughter. "You okay, sweetie?"

"I'm singing to Noël. Remember the song we learned in church school? *Little donkey, little donkey, on the dusty road. Got to keep on plodding onward...*"

Holly heard Grady make a low moaning sound.

Afraid the motion was doing further damage, she shushed Brianna and leaned down so she could hear him better. "Is something hurting you?"

"Shinging. Besh knew it." The words were distorted but recognizable as he chanted, *"With your preshous load."*

A sense of awe spread through Holly. The elderly man was freezing and in pain but he still wanted to join in the Christmas carol.

Holly nodded to Brianna and added her voice to the song, taking a gasping breath between every other word. *"Been a long time, little donkey, through the winter's night."*

"Don't give up now, little donkey," they sang together with Grady's mumble providing the bass line.

"Thank goodness!" Holly said, catching the sound of a high-pitched siren in the distance. "That's the ambulance!" She tightened her grip on Grady's jacket. "You can go a little faster, Brianna."

"Bethlehem's in sight." Brianna finished the verse and started the chorus, matching her tempo to the donkey's quicker gait. *"Ring out those bells tonight! Bethlehem, Bethlehem! Follow that star tonight!"*

Holly could see the flashing red lights reflecting on the snow as the ambulance shrieked down the highway. "Grady, we're almost there. Keep singing, Brianna!"

Brianna started the verse over again and Grady chimed in. Holly saved her breath and strength. Her arms were shaking with fatigue and her thigh muscles were quivering with the effort of breaking through the deep snow on the side of the trail. She willed the ambulance to hurry up the driveway so someone with medical expertise could look at Grady. She hoped she hadn't done the wrong thing in moving him.

They had about twenty feet to go when the ambulance rolled slowly by the fence with its window open, as an EMT peered out toward the nativity scene.

"Over here," Holly shouted. "We have him on a donkey."

The vehicle crunched to a stop and all the doors flew open, disgorging four EMTs, dressed in parkas and boots. "Mrs. Snedegar, we'll be right there," one assured her as they pulled out a backboard and raced through the gate.

"Hold on tight to Noël," Holly said to her daughter, afraid the flurry of movement would spook the donkey. But Noël kept plodding onward through the snow, just like the little creature in the song.

The EMTs jogged up to surround Noël and Grady. "We've got him now. You can let go."

She had to order her fingers to unclench from the fabric of Grady's jacket. She flexed her hands and rolled her shoulders as she hurried to where Brianna stood at Noël's head.

Holly felt tears well in her eyes as she looked into the donkey's deep brown eyes. Without a thought, she put her arms around Noël's neck and laid her cheek against the donkey's. "What a wonderful girl you are. You deserve all the apples and carrots you can eat."

"Mama, I can't believe you're hugging her," Brianna said.

Holly gave a wavering laugh as she released her hold. "I had to say thank you." She put her arm around Brianna's shoulders and gave them a squeeze. "You were amazing too."

One of the EMTs detached himself from the group carrying Grady. "Mrs. Snedegar, I'm Bob Neathawk. Can you come with us in the ambulance and tell us what happened?"

"I wish I could but I have two children and a donkey to take care of." Holly had one arm around Brianna and the other on Noël's neck. "I don't know much, so I'll tell you everything right now."

As she started to give Bob a description of how she'd found Grady by the shepherd, the beating sound of helicopter rotors swelled in volume until she couldn't make herself heard over the noise. She and Bob looked skyward to see a bright red chopper roar low over the field and up to Grady's barn where it traced a tight circle.

A police car came bouncing up the farm's road at high speed, bottoming out in one of the ruts with a bang. It screeched to a stop and Pete jumped out, shouting and pointing to where the helicopter was hovering lower and lower. "Take him up to the barn. The road over Bear Paw Mountain's all blocked up with the snow from last night, so Robbie's going to fly Grady to the regional hospital. He's going to land behind the barn where the snow's not as deep."

The EMTs were loading Grady into the ambulance as Holly and Brianna led Noël through the gate. "Pete, can you take Noël and Brianna while I ride in the ambulance to fill them in on Grady's condition?" Holly asked. She didn't want to leave Brianna and the brave little donkey but she was worried that Kayleigh would be frightened by all the activity and noise. She felt pulled in too many different directions, but she trusted Pete.

"You go," Pete said, coming over to stand beside Brianna.

Holly nodded and ran to the back of the ambulance, climbing in just as the EMT was about to close the doors.

The vehicle started forward and Holly squeezed into one corner to stay out of the way of the technicians as they began working on Grady. Bob asked her questions about how Grady looked when she found him. "I wasn't sure if I should move him," she said, "but he was so cold. I thought he needed warmth."

"You did the right thing, Mrs. Snedegar," Bob said.

"What's he saying?" another EMT asked, his ear next to Grady's mouth.

Holly scooted in closer and smiled as she caught Grady's voice. "He's singing a Christmas carol. The one about the little donkey."

She found Grady's cold hand and gave it a gentle squeeze. "Noël brought you through safely, Grady.

She didn't give up."

"Good little donkey," Grady muttered, one side of his mouth twisting upward in a smile before his eyelids fluttered closed.

Holly let go of him and sat back so the EMTs could continue to work on Grady. The ambulance bounced and swayed up the road, coming to a halt beside the barn. Holly jumped out and started toward the house where she could see Kayleigh standing in the doorway, still wearing her parka. As soon as the girl caught sight of her mother, she darted outside and into Holly's arms. "Mama, is Mr. Boone going to be okay?" Kayleigh yelled over the helicopter's racket.

"A lot of people are going to try to make him okay." Holly had learned not to make promises she had no control over keeping.

"Can we go see the helicopter?"

Since Holly wanted desperately to see Robbie, even if just for a moment, she nodded and took Kayleigh's hand, jogging to catch up with the EMTs carrying Grady. As they rounded the corner of the barn, a wall of sound and swirling snow crashed into them. Holly squinted against the snowflakes caught up in the wash of the rotors, catching sight of Robbie shoving open the big side door of the helicopter he'd carried Santa in not too long ago. Since the rotors were still turning, he ducked low to run out toward the approaching EMTs.

Her breath hitched in her chest as she took in the breadth of his shoulders and the air of authority he wore. She would try to remember him looking exactly this way when he had left for Atlanta and his new life there.

Pain and joy twisted together in her chest. This man had found her beautiful and desirable. He had wanted her enough to set aside his scruples for one glorious night. And she was going to lose him.

As he came closer, he saw her. She knew it because his expression transformed from cop to lover. She could see the blue of his eyes blaze brighter and his lips begin to soften into a smile. But he must have remembered their parting, and his face went back to cop as he nodded and added his grip to the backboard, before turning away toward the helicopter.

She and Kayleigh watched as Robbie directed the EMTs in loading the stretcher and strapping it down inside the chopper. Then he slammed the door shut and jogged back to open the pilot's door. He lifted his hand in farewell before he leapt into the seat and the helicopter lifted and banked away in a maelstrom of wind and sound.

The way he'd looked at her for that tiny moment sent joy spinning through her. It would have to be enough for a lifetime.

"Mama!" Holly spun around at the sound of Brianna's voice. She and Pete were trudging toward her with Noël plodding alongside them. Brianna handed Noël's lead line to Pete and bolted toward Holly, running up and throwing her arms around her mother's waist before bursting into tears.

Holly's throat tightened and she pulled Brianna away just enough so she could kneel down to see her tear-stained face. "What is it, sweetie? What's wrong?"

Brianna gulped on a sob. "I was so scared I was going to do something wrong and Mr. Boone would fall off Noël. But Noël was so good and did everything I asked her to."

"You were perfect and so was Noël." Holly pulled her daughter into a hug. She saw Kayleigh watching and reached out to pull her into the embrace. "So were you, Kayleigh. You were both such brave girls."

As Kayleigh joined the hug, Holly lost her balance and they all tumbled into the snow in a heap. That started them laughing so hard they didn't know if the tears on their faces were happy or sad or a little bit of both.

"I'm sorry, Pete." Holly sat up and wiped her cheeks as the police officer patiently held the donkey. "I think we needed to blow off some tension, now that Grady's safely on his way to the hospital."

Pete offered his hand to pull her to her feet. "You don't have to apologize for a thing. You and your girls just saved a man's life."

"All we did was help our friend." Holly shivered and brushed at the snow clinging to her sweater.

"This must be your jacket, ma'am." One of the EMTs approached from the ambulance, holding out the parka and scarf she'd wrapped around Grady.

Holly thanked him and slipped into the jacket. He gave her a little salute. "That was good thinking, putting Mr. Boone on a donkey to get him out of the field. In a case like this, every second counts, so getting him to us for treatment more quickly was critical."

He turned back to the ambulance, climbing in the passenger seat before it bounced away down the road.

"He's right," Pete said. "You all deserve a medal."

Brianna gave the donkey's neck a stroke. "Including Noël."

"I know something Noël would like better than a medal," Holly said. "There's a bowl of apples on Mr. Boone's kitchen table. I think he'd want Noël to have one as a reward, so why don't you girls go get one and bring it to the barn?"

"Yes, ma'am." Brianna and Kayleigh dashed away toward the house, their pink and purple boots flashing bright against the snow.

"Let's take Noël back to her stall," Holly said to Pete. As they walked through the barn door, Holly's legs suddenly turned to rubber. "I think I need to sit down," she said, stumbling over to a hay bale in the corner and collapsing onto it. She propped her elbows on her knees and dropped her head into her hands. All the emotions she'd been holding at bay so she could get Grady to safety came boiling up and her body began to shake.

"You okay?" Pete asked.

Holly nodded into her hands. "Just a delayed reaction. You go ahead with Noël."

Fear for Grady's life, terror of Noël's hooves and teeth, joy at her passion for Robbie, pain at its imminent loss, pride in her daughters. The feelings swirled and grabbed and pounded at her chest, as the muscles in her legs and arms ached with fatigue and her damp sweater clung to her skin.

But she found something underneath the vortex, something solid and calm. It was her center, the foundation she thought she'd lost under Frank's emotional battering. That was where she'd found the strength to overcome her fear of Noël, to haul Grady out of the cold snow, to hold him on the donkey's back.

And there was more there, enough to find a way to love Robbie.

As her children came through the barn door with apples cupped in their small hands, she pushed herself off the hay bale and walked with them to the donkey's stall. Pete had refilled the hay net and the water bucket, and Noël was munching contentedly once again.

Holly thought of her sister Claire who'd known what she wanted to do with her life from an early age and pursued it with a steely desire. Her sister had found a Thoroughbred for her whisper horse. And Julia's fiery artistic temperament had matched her with a giant black stallion. But Holly wasn't driven or flashy; she was simple and sturdy. That made Noël the perfect creature to help her understand herself.

She'd been given a whisper donkey to show her strength came in small, unassuming packages, and that worked for her.

"Let's go in." Holly unlatched the door.

"But you told us—" Kayleigh stopped when Brianna made a shushing gesture.

"Noël would never hurt us," Holly said. "She's my whisper donkey."

Brianna gave a little gasp. Holly looked down to find her daughter's eyes shining.

"Let me cut those apples up so Noël can eat them more easily," Pete said, pulling a pocket knife out of his back pocket.

The girls handed him their apples one at a time, and he handed them back neat slices.

Holly took a slice from Brianna and walked up to Noël. The donkey flicked her ears forward and stopped chewing on the hay. Holly flattened her hand palm up and laid the apple slice on top of it. Noël stretched out her neck and reached for the apple, pulling her lips back from her big square teeth. A flicker of nervousness dancing up Holly's arm but she took another step closer, extending her hand to Noël. The donkey lipped up the fruit and crunched it between her teeth.

Holly wrapped her arms around Noël's warm, furry neck and murmured in her ear, "Thank you for giving me back my strength."

Even when Noël lifted her head and let out one of her eardrum-bashing brays, Holly didn't let go.

CHAPTER THIRTEEN

Holly stood at the kitchen sink, rinsing out the candy cane-patterned mug she'd just drunk her nighttime tea from. The girls were in bed, exhausted after the drama-filled day, and she was close to being asleep on her feet.

Robbie had called from the hospital to say that Grady's loss of consciousness was probably due to a mild stroke. The farmer had also sprained his ankle when he fell. After some rehabilitation, the doctor was optimistic Grady would recover full speech and mobility. Relief had made Holly sag into a kitchen chair before she relayed the good news to Brianna and Kayleigh.

It had been both heaven and torture to have Robbie's voice vibrating in her ear over the phone. Not that he'd referred to what was between them; he'd simply been considerate enough to put her mind to rest about Grady. It didn't matter what his words were; it reminded her of having him whispering in her ear as they made love, telling her how beautiful and sexy she was.

Shaking her head, she turned the mug upside down and set it on the drying rack. She jumped when the doorbell rang. Frowning at the clock, which read 9:30, she dried her hands on the plaid dishtowel and wondered who would be calling at this hour. For a moment, she felt a quiver of nerves that it might be Frank, but the anxiety died as quickly as it had been born. She'd lost her fear of him today, too.

She went to the door and peeked through the sidelight. Standing on the front porch, his hands shoved into the pockets of his police jacket, was Robbie. He stood with his legs apart and his head lowered. The porch light glinted on his badge and the polished tips of his boots.

Every atom of her body leapt and yearned toward him, but his stance was tense and somber, sending a frisson of disquiet up her spine. Had Grady taken an unexpected turn for the worse?

She smoothed her palms on the side of her jeans and pulled the door open. "Hey, Robbie. Is everything all right with Grady?"

He raised his head and nodded. "Grady's going to be fine." He stared at her for a moment, almost as though he was trying to memorize her face. "Can I come in for a few minutes?"

"Sure." She stepped back to let him pass. It felt awkward not to touch him, seeing as she'd explored every inch of his body the night before. "Would you like some pie or something warm to drink?"

"No, thanks. Are the girls asleep?" He glanced

over her shoulder as though looking for them.

"Yes, they were exhausted. Come on in and sit down." She led the way to the living room where the Christmas tree's lights glowed in all their colors and three quilted stockings dangled from the greenery-laden mantel.

Robbie walked to the unlit fireplace. He stared into it for a long moment, then pivoted to look her in the eye. "I have to ask you something I have no right to." She saw the muscles in his throat move as he swallowed.

"What is it?" She hated to see him look so unhappy.

"You saved Grady's life today."

Why would that make him miserable? "A lot of people pitched in," she said. "Even Noël helped."

"You're an amazing woman. A beautiful woman." He paced away a few steps before returning his gaze to her. "I realized something today." He swallowed again. "I love you."

His words seemed to spin inside her chest, throwing off sparkles of warmth. She wanted to leap into his arms, but he stood stiffly, as though this brought him no pleasure, so she held herself still. She opened her mouth to tell him she loved him right back but he held up his hand to stop her.

"I know what your answer will be, but I have to ask," he said. "Would you come to Atlanta with me? As my wife?"

She'd often told him she couldn't imagine leaving Sanctuary because all of her support was here. Her sister Claire, who had sold her most precious possession to give Holly the security of owning her home. Claire's solid, steady husband Tim who had helped rescue Brianna and Kayleigh when Frank had kidnapped them. Paul Taggart, who had handled all the legal problems of her divorce with such kindness. Her fellow moms who had brought food and offered free babysitting in the grim days after Frank fled with all her money. In Atlanta there would be no safety net.

She looked at the man in front of her, his eyes holding all she wanted for her future. And she made the leap, knowing he would always be there to catch her.

"Yes!" she yelped. "Yes, I'll marry you and go to Timbuktu if you want to." She hurled herself at him, wanting to kiss him so badly it was a physical ache.

He caught her with a look of such disbelief that she laughed, giddy with the joy of knowing he loved her as much as she loved him.

"Are you sure?" he asked, even as his arms came around her like warm bands of steel. "I know how you feel about uprooting Brianna and Kayleigh after all they've been through."

She thought of Brianna leading Noël through the snow, and Kayleigh sitting alone in Grady's house while helicopters and ambulances roared past. Her daughters were strong women too. "They'll love the adventure. We all will."

He dropped his forehead onto her shoulder with a groan that sounded like it came from deep in his soul. "I didn't dare to hope…I can't believe…" She felt a shudder run through him before he lifted his head. The blue of his eyes seemed to glow. "If you said no to Atlanta, I was going to turn down the job. I couldn't leave you."

She slipped her arms inside his jacket and wrapped them around his waist. "I would never ask you to do that."

"You're an incredible woman," he said.

"You know what incredible women really like?" She gave him her most flirtatious look.

His hold on her tightened so she was pressed against his body from chest to knee. "What's that?"

"To be kissed."

He bent his head and brought his lips close to hers. "Remember that imaginary hedge of mistletoe I mentioned last night?"

"Yes."

"Make it a forest." He pulled her in and kissed her as though he was never going to stop.

CHAPTER FOURTEEN

"Mama, look at all the cars!" Kayleigh said from the back seat of the minivan.

"This is more than last year," Brianna chimed in.

"A lot more," Holly said, joining the line of vehicles being directed by a squad of policemen in yellow traffic vests waving flashing batons. "Look! They've cleared the field for people to park in."

She followed Tim and Claire's big SUV into the plowed cornfield across the highway from Grady Boone's farm. Another policeman waved them into an empty space beside her sister's car.

Brianna and Kayleigh tumbled out of the minivan, the silver threads in their knitted hats glinting in the constant stream of headlights. Holly was still zipping up her parka when Kayleigh raced up to the nearest police officer. "Is Captain Robbie here?"

"He's the boss, so he's most likely out on the highway," the cop said. "But don't go there without your parents."

Holly recognized the young man. "Sam, where on earth did all these cars come from?"

Sam waved another minivan into a vacant spot. "Well, word kind of spread about a heroic little donkey and a special nativity scene." He looked down at Brianna and Kayleigh. "I hear there's some extra-good hot chocolate across the street."

A little jab of guilt hit Holly. At the meeting to organize Christmas Eve refreshments, she'd offered to bring cookies or hot chocolate, but had been told by Bernie Weikle that she'd done enough for the nativity scene. She hadn't known how to overrule the forceful Mrs. Weikle, so she'd come empty-handed.

Claire and Tim strolled up beside her. "Wow, the Christmas Eve nativity scene tradition just got a lot bigger," Claire said, surveying the mass of cars and people. "Thank goodness, Captain Robbie is on top of things!"

Holly couldn't quell the smile of pride that curved her lips, although her engagement to Robbie was still a secret between the two of them. She wanted to shout the news to the world but they had decided to give the news to Brianna and Kayleigh tomorrow evening as a sort of Christmas gift. Then they'd share it with family and friends. "I wonder how he knew all these people would show up."

"Like any good cop, he has his sources," Tim said.

Holly took the girls' hands and their little group

hurried along the frozen ground, stepping carefully over the stubs of cornstalks, to the gate onto the highway. Robbie's best friend Pete was shepherding pedestrians across the road. "Merry Christmas Eve!" he greeted them.

"And the same to you," Holly said, as the crowd surged across the asphalt. "Is Robbie here?"

Pete shook his head. "But he'll be back. He had to pick up a package."

"A package?"

"Or maybe he said a special delivery." Pete grinned and went back to directing traffic. He gave her a little salute as she crossed the road, keeping a firm grip on her children's small, mittened hands.

"I wish Mr. Boone was here," Brianna said, her eyes wide as she took in the crowd stretched out along the highway.

A twinge of sadness hit her at her daughter's words. She hated to think of Grady being in the hospital over Christmas. "Me too, sweetie. Mrs. Weikle has promised him a copy of the news video she's going to shoot tonight, so at least he'll get to see it." She'd made Bernie promise to leave her out of the video though.

"Bri! Kayleigh! Merry Christmas Eve!" A group of little girls squealed as they caught sight of her daughters. "We saw the brave little donkey. She's kind of small, but really cute. Come get hot chocolate with us!"

"We're going to see the nativity scene first," Holly said.

"Okay, Mrs. Snedegar. We'll see you later." The girls whirled off up Grady's farm road to where the food trucks were parked. From somewhere in that same direction, the sound of *Away in a Manger* being sung by amateur but enthusiastic voices made her smile.

She let Tim and Claire go first since her giant brother-in-law easily cleared a path through the spectators. As she walked along the side of the road toward the field where a glow of light arched up against the clear, starry sky, friends and neighbors called out holiday greetings. She and her girls smiled and waved and kept walking.

Everywhere she looked, people were smiling and hugging and wishing each other a happy holiday. Despite the numbers, there was no jostling or shoving.

As they reached the nativity field, Tim found an empty spot along the fence and squeezed the two little girls in. He waved Holly into the space just behind them.

There, lit by floodlights that made the newly-painted figures glow brilliantly against the snow, was the restored nativity scene.

One of the neighboring farmers had volunteered to take care of Grady's livestock while he was in the hospital. Evidently, the farmer had decided to add his own animals to the spectacle because there were several sheep, a goat, a horse, and a dog in a doghouse, in addition to Grady's cow Flo and the chickens.

But in the place of honor, placidly munching her hay at a manger set up right beside the Virgin Mary, stood Noël, wearing her green-and-red plaid blanket and a big red bow around her neck.

"Noël looks so pretty," Brianna said. "I wish we could go pet her."

"We'll bring her some Christmas carrots tomorrow," Holly said.

As the person beside them moved away, Claire stepped up to the fence while Tim stood behind her with his arms wrapped around her waist. "It looks amazing, Holl," she said. "Even better than before."

"It does look nice," Holly said, "but what's even nicer is all these people brought together on Christmas Eve. That's what I wanted to keep."

The wail of a siren broke through the laughter and conversation of the crowd. Everyone turned to watch a police cruiser and an ambulance make their way through the police barricades to turn into the farm road.

"It's Robbie," Holly breathed, recognizing his car. Happiness surged through her in a warm wave, even as she wondered who had the misfortune to require the ambulance. Needing to get closer to her fiancé, she turned to Claire. "Would you mind taking Brianna and Kayleigh for a minute?"

"Of course not," her sister said. "Go see what's happening."

Holly jogged past the onlookers until she reached the two parked vehicles. The back door of the ambulance was open and a wheelchair sat on the road beside it. Robbie stood by the wheelchair, his gaze on the medical technicians leaning into the emergency vehicle.

Holly walked up beside him, just barely stopping herself from taking his hand. "Is someone hurt?" she asked.

He didn't feel any such constraint because he slipped his arm around her waist and pulled her against his side, looking down at her with such love in his face that she nearly gasped with the joy of it. "We brought Grady back to Sanctuary for Christmas. It didn't seem right for everyone to be here without him, and the doc has arranged for all the medical care he needs in his house for the next two days. Grady was so happy, he practically jumped out of his hospital bed."

The technicians emerged with a bundled-up Grady supported between them and helped him into the wheelchair. Holly knelt beside the farmer and kissed him gently on the cheek. "It's so good to have you back. This is the best Christmas gift ever."

"I had to make sure that young whippersnapper Purvis was taking good care of Noël and Flo." Holly was relieved to hear that his speech was only slightly slurred.

"They look just fine," she said. "And you've got quite a crowd tonight."

Grady shook his head in wonder. "I wish Bess could see this. She'd be that chuffed."

"Mr. Boone!" Brianna and Kayleigh ran up to the wheelchair with Claire and Tim following behind. "We wanted you to be back for Christmas."

Grady's face lit up. "And here I am."

"Will you come to our house tomorrow for Christmas Day?" Kayleigh asked Grady. She looked up at Holly. "It's okay to invite him, isn't it?"

"It wouldn't be Christmas without him." Holly smiled up into Robbie's eyes for a fleeting moment. "Captain Robbie will be with us too."

"I don't want to get in the way of your celebration," Grady said, but his face told another tale.

Holly shook her head. "I think Noël would be disappointed if you didn't come. She worked hard to get us all together."

"Then I reckon I'll join you, if the doc says yes," the old farmer allowed.

"Okay, let's get you over to see how the nativity scene looks," Robbie said.

The wheelchair couldn't roll over the snow-covered gravel but there was no lack of strong, willing arms to carry it to the smooth pavement of the highway. Robbie took Holly's hand and drew her along with him as he signaled his officers to hold the traffic while Grady was wheeled along the edge of Route 60. Brianna and Kayleigh walked on either side of the farmer, occasionally waving to their friends, while the med tech stood aside to let Robbie take over pushing the farmer.

As their little procession trundled along, a low murmur began to ripple through the spectators who lined the fence. Someone started clapping, the gloved hands making a strange, muffled applause. Soon the sound rose from one end of the crowd to the other and people called out, "Thank you, Mr. Boone! Merry Christmas!" as he passed.

"Well, I'll be doggoned," Grady muttered.

As they came to a spot directly in front of the nativity scene, Robbie turned the wheelchair. Once again, helpers sprang forward to lift the chair over the snow and carry Grady to the fence. Brianna and Kayleigh stood on either side of the wheelchair, pointing out to the farmer which figures they'd painted.

Standing behind Grady and the girls, Robbie wrapped his arm around Holly's waist and said, "This is one heck of a first Christmas together."

Holly snuggled in closer to him. "And we'll take all this love with us wherever we go."

EPILOGUE

Not quite two years later

"That son of yours has quite a set of lungs," Tim said, bending down to peer at Robert Boone McGraw where he rested in the crook of Holly's arm. "Reverend Hibbert jumped about a foot when Boone started to wail after the holy water dripped on his forehead."

"The only voice louder than Boone's is Noël's," Holly agreed, adjusting the white blanket that swaddled her newly baptized son. She glanced around Grady's barn to see if the donkey was in sight, but couldn't find her amongst all the party guests.

Tim ran his finger down Boone's cheek, making the baby reach for his huge hand. "You know, it's become quite a tradition in this town to have large four-footed animals at family celebrations. I'm glad you and Robbie continued it."

Holly was happy they had come back to Sanctuary to have their baby son baptized. When she'd asked Grady if they could hold the reception in his barn, the old farmer had been pleased as punch. Julia had supervised the decorating and her artist's eye showed in every corner. The barn was lit by strands of tiny white lights and dotted with giant pots of fall flowers sitting atop hay bales. "I can't imagine a nicer place to have a party, and it seemed right to have Noël present. Boone might not be here without her." She gazed down into her month-old baby's face, lit by the startlingly blue eyes his father had handed down, and felt such an up-swelling of love she thought she might not be able to breathe.

As if on cue, Robbie walked up to slip his arm around her waist, his eyes also on his new son. "That boy gets better looking every minute."

"I can't argue that because he looks just like you." Holly nestled up against her husband's side. He looked as handsome in his blue suit as he did in his police uniform. Not that he wore a uniform anymore; he'd made detective in Atlanta in record time.

Claire joined the group, and Tim spread his fingers over the slight bump showing under her green silk tunic. "I can't wait to meet this one," he said, his face softening.

"I'm going to get a lot fatter before that happens." Claire put her own hand over her husband's.

"Do you have any names picked out?" Robbie

asked.

"We're thinking 'Venetia' if it's a girl." Tim grinned at his wife.

Claire gave her husband a gentle elbow in the ribs. "He's only saying that because we think the baby was conceived in Venice."

"In a gondola on the Grand Canal," Tim elaborated.

"Too much information," Holly said.

A flurry of barking and a loud hee-haw interrupted the conversation. Holly peered through the crowd to see Adam Bosch's black German Shepherd Trace dancing around Noël's hooves. A slim blonde woman raced up to grab the dog's collar, saying, "Sit, Trace," in a stern voice. The glossy black dog instantly put his haunches on the ground and began licking her arm. "I'm sorry, everyone," Hannah Linden, Tim's partner at the veterinary hospital said, her fair skin flushed with embarrassment. "Trace forgot his party manners when he saw a real, live donkey."

A tall, dark man and a teenaged boy joined Hannah. Adam Bosch stroked the dog's head before his son Matt took a firm grip on his collar and hauled him away. Adam listened attentively as Hannah said something emphatic to her new husband before he threw back his head and laughed.

"I've never seen Adam laugh like that before," Holly said. She'd talked to the famous chef on the phone as they planned the menu for Boone's christening party, but she hadn't seen him in a social setting since she and Robbie moved to Atlanta.

"Hannah's changed him," Tim said.

"And Matt," Claire said. "She's chased away the shadows from both their lives. With Satchmo's help, of course."

Robbie let go of Holly and held out his arms for Boone. "Why don't you get something to eat? I want to show off my son."

As Holly transferred their child to Robbie's strong grasp, she met his eyes. What she saw in them squeezed the breath out of her lungs all over again. She decided she owed Noël a special treat for showing her she was ready to take the risk of loving this incredible man and giving him the chance to love her back without any regret for what his life might have been.

Holly inspected the buffet table, finding a platter of cheese and sliced apples and a tray of crudités. She snagged some carrots and apples and wrapped them in a napkin.

Armed with her treats, she made a circuit of the barn. Noël was nowhere in sight. "Who are you looking for?" Julia asked as Holly passed by the artist and her lawyer husband.

"My whisper donkey." Holly opened up the napkin.

Paul rolled his eyes, but with a grin. "Another one drinks the Kool-Aid. Does Sharon Sydenstricker recognize whisper donkeys in her mythology?"

Holly nodded. "She gave Noël her seal of approval, so my donkey has been admitted to the official Society of Whisper Horses."

"So there," Julia said to her husband before turning back to Holly. "Don't let him bother you. He's the one who dragged me into Sharon's stable in my fancy evening clothes so he could propose to me outside Darkside's stall. He was afraid I wouldn't marry him if my whisper horse wasn't in on the deal."

"I'm pretty sure I carried you in because you didn't want to ruin your shoes." Paul mussed his wife's bright red hair. "I saw Grady lead Noël into her stall after the excitement with Trace. I'm pretty sure Brianna and Kayleigh followed him."

Holly thanked them and headed for the stall. She heard Grady's low rumble and the girls' high voices before she got there. When she unlatched the door and slipped inside, three guilty faces turned to look at her. Noël continued to chew on her hay.

"Mama, we just wanted to make sure Noël was happy." Brianna jumped up from the bale of straw where she and Kayleigh sat.

Grady levered himself up from his own bale. "Truth is we all needed a rest from the festivities."

Holly laughed and put her arm around Brianna's shoulders. "Noël deserves your company. In fact, I came to give her a special treat to say thank you."

At the sound of her voice, the donkey's head came around. The girls had created a necklace of autumn leaves and dried flowers which they'd hung around Noël's neck. They'd also tied an orange-and-brown plaid ribbon around her tail so the donkey looked quite festive.

Holly walked up and gave Noël a scratch behind her ears before she arranged a couple of apple slices on her palm. The donkey scarfed up the apple and snuffled at the napkin for the carrots . Holly handed one to Brianna and one to Kayleigh so they could treat the donkey too. "What are you thanking Noël for?" Brianna asked.

"For her strength and her wisdom."

Grady nodded. "Noël's special that way."

Holly remembered a piece of good news she'd just heard. "I hear congratulations are in order. I'm so happy for you and Bernie." She gave Grady a hug.

The old farmer actually blushed. "When she wrote that article about the nativity scene, Bernie pestered me with so many questions, she found out about my knitting. She helped me pick out colors for another baby blanket and one thing led to another."

"What about Bernie?" Kayleigh asked.

"Mr. Boone and Mrs. Weikle are getting married," Holly said.

Brianna and Kayleigh looked surprised. "But Mrs. Weikle is old," Kayleigh said.

At that, Grady started to chuckle, a deep rusty rasp. "So'm I."

Kayleigh nodded. "I know, but it's not polite to say so."

That made Grady laugh so hard, he had to get out his handkerchief to wipe his eyes. "I sure do miss you girls since you moved down to Atlanta."

Brianna turned to Holly. "Can we tell him our

news?"

"Not without me." Robbie opened the stall door and walked in with Boone. "Someone told me my whole family was hiding out in Noël's stall."

"We're not hiding, Daddy," Kayleigh explained. "We're keeping Noël company."

"It seems kind of appropriate to have a baby and a donkey in a stable." Holly moved to kiss Boone's fat little cheek. The baby blinked sleepily at her.

"Now can we tell him?" Brianna asked.

Holly nodded.

Brianna turned to Grady. "We're moving back to Sanctuary. Daddy's going to be a police chief and fly helicopters to rescue sick people, just like when you fell in the field. It's called Medevac."

"That's right good news." Grady directed a questioning gaze at Holly and Robbie. "I thought you folks were well settled down there."

"We love Atlanta." Holly meant it sincerely. The four of them had explored the city and its surroundings with excited delight. Holly had even begun to take flying lessons. But when she'd told Robbie she was pregnant, he'd kissed her and said, "Let's go home."

"Living in the city was a great adventure," she said to Grady, "but our family and friends are here."

Robbie nodded, one arm cradling his son and the other around his wife's shoulders. "Sanctuary is where our hearts live."

Author's Note

For those wonderful folks who have already read the three full-length Whisper Horse novels that were published prior to this novella, I thought you might be interested in where Holly and Robbie's story fits in chronologically. The events in *A Down-home Country Christmas* take place approximately a year and a half after Claire Parker and Tim Arbuckle fall in love in *Take Me Home,* the first book in the Whisper Horse series.

Here's a quick summary of where all the main characters from *Take Me Home, Country Roads,* and *The Place I Belong* stand when *A Down-home Country Christmas* begins:

Claire and Tim have been married for about six months, although they feel as though they are still on their honeymoon. Tim has hired an associate at his veterinary practice so he can travel with Claire for her international art dealings. However, the associate doesn't like the isolated location of Sanctuary, West Virginia, so he will resign in the next few months. Then Tim will hire Hannah Linden, the heroine of *The Place I Belong,* who chooses the job precisely because of its isolation.

Claire's whisper horse Willow has recovered fully from her emergency operation and is about to become a mother.

Julia Castillo and Paul Taggart, the protagonists of *Country Roads,* met during the summer just past and are madly in love. Paul has not yet popped the question, but everyone in Sanctuary knows it's only a matter of time before the two of them make it official. Paul's *Pro Bono* project is going like gangbusters, and Julia's new style of painting has taken the art world by storm.

Julia's whisper horse Darkside still pretends to be a cranky, dangerous stallion, but the stable hands at Healing Springs Stables know it's just an act these days. Darkside has learned to trust humans again, thanks to Julia.

In this story, Adam Bosch of *The Place I Belong* does not know he has a thirteen-year-old son named Matt nor has he met Hannah Linden since she has not yet fled from Chicago to Sanctuary (see Claire and Tim's paragraph above). Adam is still burying himself in working at his brilliantly successful restaurant The Aerie rather than facing the demons of his past.

Matt's whisper pony Satchmo is living with his stall buddy Jazzman at the racing stable in Florida.

A Down-home Country Christmas is my holiday gift to you, my fabulous readers. You close the circle for my books, so I wanted to say thank you by giving you the story you requested. Happy holidays!

ACKNOWLEDGMENTS

This novella would not be the work it is without the help of many wonderful people. I'd like to thank:

Miriam Allenson, Cathy Greenfeder, and Lisa Verge Higgins, my critique partners, for their support, encouragement, and brilliant suggestions.

Andrea Hurst, my developmental editor, for making sure I always reward my readers with the big emotional payoff.

Alastair Stephens, my copyeditor and all-around technical guru, for giving this novella its final spit-and-polish.

Rogenna Brewer, my cover designer, for capturing exactly the right feeling visually.

Jeff, Rebecca, and Loukas, my family, who keep the Christmas spirit of love glowing all year long.

ABOUT THE AUTHOR

Nancy Herkness is the author of the award-winning Wager of Hearts and Whisper Horse series, as well as several other contemporary romance novels. She has received many honors for her work, including the Book Buyers Best Top Pick Award, the Maggie Award, and the National Excellence in Romance Fiction Award, and she is a two-time nominee for the Romance Writers of America's RITA award. She graduated from Princeton University with a degree in English literature and creative writing.

A native of West Virginia, Nancy now lives in a Victorian house twelve miles west of the Lincoln Tunnel in New Jersey with her husband, two mismatched dogs, and an elderly cat.

For more information about Nancy and her books, visit www.NancyHerkness.com.

Made in the USA
Coppell, TX
18 July 2021

59141947R00098